BUTTERFLY TEARS

BUTTERFLY TEARS

STORIES BY

ZOË S. ROY

ınanna poetry & fiction series

INANNA Publications and Education Inc.
Toronto, Canada

We gratefully acknowledge the support of the Canada Council for the Arts and the Ontario Arts Council for our publishing program

The publisher is also grateful for the kind support received from an Anonymous Fund at The Calgary Foundation.

Library and Archives Canada Cataloguing in Publication

Roy, Zoë S., 1953-
        Butterfly tears : stories / by Zoë S. Roy.

(Inanna poetry and fiction series)
ISBN 978-0-9782233-7-3

        I. Title. II. Series: Inanna poetry and fiction series

PS8635.O94B88 2009   C813'.6   C2009-905066-8

Cover design by Val Fullard
Interior design by Luciana Ricciutelli
Printed and bound in Canada

Inanna Publications and Education Inc.
210 Founders College, York University
4700 Keele Street
Toronto, Ontario, Canada M3J 1P3
Telephone: (416) 736-5356 Fax (416) 736-5765
Email: inanna@yorku.ca
Website: www.yorku.ca/inanna

Posthumously dedicated to my parents who provided a reading environment that stimulated my interest in literature, even though, following the rationale of the time, they tried to steer me toward science to avoid any form of persecution.

CONTENTS

Butterfly Tears
1

Wild Onions
17

Yearning
29

Frog Fishing
43

A Woman of China
51

Ten Yuan
63

Balloons
71

Twin Rivers
85

VII

Herbs
101

A Mandarin Duck
115

Noodles
129

Gingko
137

Fortune-Telling
151

Life Insurance
157

Jing and the Caterpillar
171

Acknowledgements
177

BUTTERFLY TEARS

Friday night, after tucking her five-year-old daughter in bed, Sunni tried to relax on the couch, looking for something easy to watch on television. The mahogany clock on the wall struck ten. Her husband, Paul, was late. *Is he helping his students with their assignments again?* She drew a breath, then curled her legs beneath her on the couch. A co-worker's gossip popped stubbornly into her head. *Could Paul be having an affair? Like her colleague's husband was?* She shook her head as if that could get rid of this unpleasant notion.

She flipped her loose, black hair over her shoulders and stretched her arm to turn on the radio sitting on an end table. It was Radio McGill's international music hour. She found listening to the radio deeply relaxing. As she immersed herself in the music, she closed her eyes, and allowed her mind to wander. To her surprise, she heard a familiar violin solo composed by a Chinese musician she had always been partial to. It was one of her favourites: "Liang and Zhu, Forever Lovers." The melody was an unhurried breeze on a hot and damp night, slipping through the window and filling the air like the heady aroma of rich coffee. Sunni sank into the music's sweetness as the memories it triggered played in her mind.

***

Over three decades earlier on a summer afternoon in Guilin, China, five-year-old Sunni stood on a pile of red bricks that sat under a win of Guilin University's largest one-storey dormitory. She leaned her small forehead against the windowpane, eyes wide open, trying to make out what Crazy Wen, the only person in the room, was doing. But the glass was dusty, and a blanket hanging haphazardly from the inside partially covered the window, obstructing her view.

"Sunni! Come down," ordered a young boy from behind. "Your grandma's calling you home," he urged, tugging at the worn corner of her favourite white blouse.

Startled, Sunni toppled off the brick pile, dropping onto the ground, somewhat dazed and irritated. "Lei! You scared me," she shouted, glaring at the boy standing over her outstretched body.

"Sorry. But your – yourrr – grr – grrr – graandma's looking for you," Lei sputtered, pulling Sunni to her feet.

It was precisely at that moment that Sunni detected the aching strings of a violin wafting from the nearby window. It was the first time she ever heard a violin. The sound was different from that of her father's harmonica. The music was sharp and sad, which touched her heart. Remembering her grandmother, she hurried toward home, which was in another smaller dormitory just across the road. The melody of the violin chased her down the street as she ran. Its beauty stamped itself indelibly in her mind as much as the violinist who teased those sounds from the bow held tenderly in his hand.

Crazy Wen, who majored in Music Composition at Guilin University, was a teaching assistant in the Arts Department. Sunni had heard that he went crazy after his girlfriend broke up with him. Sunni had many questions running around in her mind and did not know the answers to them. She was too young to understand the complexity of human relationships; her world still revolved around the lives of her mom and dad. *What did it mean to have a girlfriend? Was it like having a mom? How did she throw Crazy Wen away? Did she really slap him when she left?*

When she was sent to stay with her grandparents, she always felt very sad to leave her mother. So she felt the same sorrow for Crazy Wen. Sunni's mother had told her she would come to get her as soon as her newborn brother was a little older. She wondered if Crazy Wen's mom would come to take him home some day.

Crazy Wen had ear hair and a floating goatee, which made him look like a civil servant in Chinese historical war movies. Whenever Sunni went to the cafeteria at the university with her grandmother for steam buns or played with other children on the campus playground, she would see him wandering aimlessly down the road, never talking to anybody. When Crazy Wen confined himself in his apartment with the door and windows closed for several days, she felt as if he had disappeared from the world. He always wore a loose white shirt and faded black slacks, and his goatee bounced lightly back and forth when he strolled through the campus. Curious children always followed him, imitating his funny stroll. Sunni sometimes joined them, her heart pounding when she caught up to him and found herself walking just behind him. Always on alert, she was ready to run should he turn and threaten to chase her. He never did, though. Maybe he didn't care whether the children followed him or not.

Since the time Sunni first heard the violin music drifting from Wen's apartment she had stopped following him, although she still felt curious about him, and still thought about his "mom," and why she'd left him, too.

One day, while her grandmother sorted soybean sprouts, Sunni snuggled in close to her and asked, "Why did Crazy Wen's girlfriend give him a slap?"

"Oh, dear! Who told you Crazy Wen got slapped?" Amused by Sunni's question, her grandmother explained, "His girlfriend doubted his musical ability and left him to marry a man who had been selected for further studies in music in the Soviet Union."

"What did Crazy Wen do?"

"He became crazy, and that is how he got his nickname," she chuckled.

"What's that song he always plays?"

"That's a composition," her grandmother said. "It's the story of Liang and Zhu."

"Who are Liang and Zhu?"

"You ask too many questions," her grandmother chided, as she thought about how to answer. "A long time ago, a girl named Zhu disguised herself as a boy so she could go to school."

"Why did she wear boy's clothes?"

3

"Well, because at that time, girls were not allowed to go to school."

"Why weren't girls allowed to go to school?"

"Don't interrupt me. It is just the way it was," her grandmother scolded, dropping a handful of the selected soybean sprouts absentmindedly into the bowl at her feet. "One day Zhu met a man named Liang on the way to school. They fell madly in love with each other, and were a really good match."

Sunni watched her grandmother carefully select more sprouts as she listened to the story.

"But Zhu's family thought Liang's family was too poor. They wanted to marry Zhu into a rich and powerful family. And a marriage had already been arranged for her – "

"So what happened?" Sunni asked breathlessly, holding her grandmother's arm as tight as she could.

"Liang became very sick. He never recovered and died."

"Died?" Sunni gasped. She shook her grandmother's arm and asked, "How come Grandma? Why didn't he go to hospital?"

"Don't shake my arm, little one," her grandmother said. "My bean sprouts are all falling onto the floor. There were no hospitals at that time," she sighed, as she bent to pick up the fallen sprouts. "Heartbroken, Zhu insisted on visiting Liang's grave on the way to the wedding her parents had arranged for her."

"Did she get to see his grave?"

"Yes, she did. And as she approached, Liang's grave suddenly opened, and Zhu jumped in. Just as suddenly, the grave closed over them both."

"Did she really jump into the grave?" Sunni asked, trying to imagine what an open grave looked like.

"Yes, so the story goes. Liang and Zhu became two beautiful butterflies in their next lives." Her grandmother's voice got a little louder. "The two butterflies met every day over the grave. Their love was predestined."

After learning the story of Liang and Zhu, Sunni could picture the two butterflies dancing over the grave whenever she heard Crazy Wen play his violin – and that piercing melody would become the grey cloud of her childhood.

***

The radio drew Sunni back to the present. A couple of hours had passed but Paul had not yet returned. The pleasure of listening to music dissolved.

Ten minutes later, Sunni went to bed. She tossed and turned, dreaming that a car with high beams unexpectedly dashed toward her while she was slowly crossing a street. She jumped onto a sidewalk, but could not elude the car. Although she ran behind a fence, the car continued to follow her closely, like a cat chasing its own tail. To escape, Sunni pushed open the door of a shopping mall that appeared conveniently in front of her. In the blink of an eye, however, all the lights went out, and she suddenly found herself at the edge of a steep cliff. She did not have time to stop, and her feet slipped off the cliff. Her body floated in the air. "Help!" she tried to shout, but no sound came out. Finally, she was able to grab hold of a branch from a small, jutting tree and climb back onto the bluff.

Paul came home in the wee hours of the morning. The moment he slipped in next to her, Sunni stretched her arm out to grip his as if it were the branch that helped her climb to safety in her dream. Startled, he asked, "What's the matter with you?" But Sunni did not respond. Irritated, Paul drew back his arm and pulled the blanket up to his shoulders.

Sunni turned over, caught in the web of her dream where she hovered in the air like a large, sleek bird. She spotted a dark, green river flowing slowly through the fields and forests beneath her. Several fish hawks were diving into the water while a few bamboo fishing-punts moved smoothly in the river, and picturesque hills formed in limestone karst soaring alongside. Fog like a veil gently wrapped itself around these variously shaped hills, their reflections in the water occasionally shaking with ripples. Sunni flew past The Hill of Waiting for Husband, a hill that looked like a woman standing in mourning over the river; a woman who had turned into stone after years of waiting for her husband to return home from the war. Just then, a song echoed around the hills:

Flowers grow on a mountain top,
The fragrance drifts below.

The water flows past beneath the bridge,
The breeze blows coolness over it.

Sunni recognized the Li River winding through the city of Guilin where her grandparents had lived. Guilin was a place of gorgeous green mountains, where the fragrance of cassia trees wafts, and tropical birds roam. She had left the city long ago and had not been back since her grandparents passed away.

Her dream took her back to many years earlier when she had walked with her playmates, swimsuits in hand, along the Li River toward Elephant Trunk Hill.

"Crazy Wen has been found!" announced one of the boys that fateful day.

"What?" Sunni stopped walking. "Where is he?" she asked with excitement and dread. She knew Crazy Wen had been missing for days.

"He's in the water near Elephant Trunk Hill," said the boy.

"Dead or alive?" Sunni asked, not able to disguise the frantic worry in her voice.

"Sure, he's dead." The boy threw his swimming suit in the air and jumped to catch it. "Dare you to go look at the body?"

"What the heck!" one of the girls shouted back. "Let's go see him!"

In the dream, Sunni stood at the foot of Elephant Trunk Hill. She could hear water being sucked into the elephant's trunk. She wondered what Crazy Wen had looked like in the water, but could not remember his appearance no matter how hard she tried. She had followed the children that day, shaking over Wen's death in a way she could never explain to anyone. The only thing she could remember was that Crazy Wen killed himself right at the beginning of the Cultural Revolution, in the chaotic summer of 1966, when everything changed. The haunting strains of the violin solo, "Liang and Zhu," broke off the moment Wen's life snapped like a violin string.

***

When morning's sunbeams streamed into the bedroom, Sunni woke with a start and sat straight up in bed. She realized she did not need go to work – it was Saturday. Her husband was sleeping like a log. She watched his face and wondered what had changed him. *The wrinkles that lined his forehead are supposed to display a man's maturity, but is Paul mature?* Now, in his early forties, he had reached a period in his life he could be proud of. He had settled into family life and had been teaching for years at the community college.

They had met seven years earlier. Sunni had found a part-time job in a public library after her graduation from the Library Science and Information Program at Concordia University. She was responsible for a section of bookshelves called Other Languages where there were many books in Chinese, Slavic, Arabic, and Japanese. Chinese books occupied almost a whole bookshelf.

Sometimes, Sunni would shelve the scattered books that had been pulled out and left by readers. One day, while she was shelf-reading, making sure all the books on the shelves were in order by checking their call numbers, a man rushed up to her and asked, "Excuse me. Can you tell me if you have this book?" He showed her a piece of paper in his hand and pointed to a title in Chinese: *Liang and Zhu.*

"No. We don't," she replied, casting a cursory glance at the books on the shelf to disguise her surprise at his request. "But I might be able to locate a copy for you," she added, turning her head slowly to meet his eyes.

"Really? Where?" the man asked. "I just feel like reading it," he said with a pleased smile, "so anytime would be fine."

"All Chinese books are circulated from the National Library among public libraries all over Canada. I'll ask for a copy and call you when it arrives."

"Great. I appreciate your help." The man took a pen and wrote down his name and phone number on a slip of paper he pulled from his pocket. "I'm Paul. Are you new here?"

Sunni nodded. "Do you use this library often?" she asked.

"Yes, I'm a regular patron and I like to read in Chinese once in a while," he replied, passing her the slip with his phone number before turning to leave.

Sunni was able to find a copy of *Liang and Zhu* for Paul. And, not long afterward, she and Paul began dating. He was an intelligent and gentle man with a wonderfully dry sense of humour. Sunni was so attracted to him that she hated the fact she hadn't met him earlier. That he had asked her to find him the story of Liang and Zhu seemed an omen that they were meant to be together.

Sunni believed she was a happy version of Zhu. It was not long before she and Paul married and had a daughter.

***

Recently, Sunni found Paul increasingly absentminded, even when they made love. She asked him what was bothering him but he would not, or could not answer. Sunni had heard about the "seven-year itch" – the vague uneasiness that arises after seven years of marriage. She wondered if her marriage was experiencing this "itch."

She stared at the alarm clock on the night table. It was just past 8:00 a.m. She had promised their daughter, Ida, they would go to a wide-screen movie at the IMAX theatre that afternoon. She dressed quickly and left Paul sleeping in the bedroom.

Ida was playing with her dolls on the couch in the living room. Her dress was slipping off her shoulder so she smiled happily when Sunni entered the room. "Mommy! Help me," she said, pointing vigorously at her back.

Sunni got on her knees and zipped up Ida's dress, brushing her forehead with a good-morning kiss. "Have you washed your face and brushed your teeth, Ida?" Sunni asked, leading her little girl toward the bathroom.

As she pushed open the door, she detected an unfamiliar scent. Paul's clothes were lying in a jumble on top of the hamper. She picked up his shirt and sniffed it: Paul's cologne was mixed with an unfamiliar scent. *Where did the other fragrance come from? Another woman?* She shuddered at the thought and felt her heart sink.

"Mommy, can I have breakfast?" Ida asked, running from the bathroom to the kitchen. Ida was already sitting expectantly at the table when Sunni joined her.

From the cupboard, Sunni took a box of Corn Flakes and Rice Krispies and placed both on the table. She set a bowl of milk and a spoon in front of her daughter. "Ida, eat anything you like."

"Mommy, I don't want milk. I just want to drink sweet water."

"As you like." Sunni passed her the sugar bowl.

Sunni moved stiffly to the telephone on the wall next to the refrigerator. She lifted the receiver, and holding the cord, pulled the phone with her into the bathroom, where she dialled an overseas number.

"Sunflower," Sunni greeted her friend with her nickname. "It's me."

"Sunni!" her friend called out with surprise and welcome in her voice. "I haven't heard from you in ages."

Sunni did not know how to begin the conversation. "What's up?" she asked, as though there were nothing bothering her at all.

"Do you remember Dalan?" asked Sunflower.

"Sure," Sunni said, mildly curious. "Why? Did something happen to her?"

"She cut her wrists!"

"What?" Sunni shivered. "Was she found in time?"

"No. I'm afraid it was too late."

"Why did she do it?"

"Her husband was having an affair with another woman, and Dalan didn't want a divorce."

"Only in China..." Sunni sighed, her voice trailing off.

Sunflower changed her tone. "Hey, these kinds of things must happen in the States, too, right?"

"What things? And just to remind you, I'm in Montreal, Canada, not the United States." Sunni was a little disappointed with her friend, who seemed not remember where Sunni lived. "Do you mean suicides?"

"Canada and the United States are on the same continent. They aren't such different countries to me. And no, not suicide. I mean extramarital affairs."

"Maybe, but people don't kill themselves just because their partners are cheating. They just get a divorce."

"Hey, Sunni, are you thinking about a divorce?" Sunflower asked with a chuckle. "Don't rush into it. We haven't met your husband yet."

"Now that you ask, can you keep a secret?" Sunni lowered her voice. "I really need a shoulder to lean on right now."

"No problem," Sunflower replied, concern in her voice.

"I'm sure Paul has another woman. But I am not sure what to do about it."

"Are you positive? Don't suspect him without evidence," Sunflower replied matter-of-factly. "The truth is people do what they want when they have freedom to do so. A rich man might well have a couple of mistresses. Good thing my hubby is poor and can't afford to have an affair even if he wants to. Anyway, nowadays nobody believes in traditional love or in long-term relationships anymore. Don't people over there feel the same way?"

"I don't think so. But I don't have the time to debate this right now. We can talk about family relationships in this society some other time."

Sunni remembered that Sunflower had always been interested in women's issues and had wanted to work with the Provincial Women's Federation. But the Federation would only hire Communist Party members. Sunflower did not get the job because she hadn't joined the Party. She got married shortly afterward.

"You have a job, don't you?" asked Sunflower.

"Yes, I do."

"If Paul is having an affair and doesn't want to stop, just divorce him. It's easy to solve the problem over there. Divorced women over there don't get a lot of pressure from families and friends to stay together, do they?"

It bothered Sunni that Sunflower kept referring to her situation as "over there." Their worlds were not so different and she resented the implication that infidelity and divorce might be somehow less significant, or trivial, for women in North America. The collapse of a marriage she felt would be painful to anyone, anywhere. She wasn't sure how to respond, so she simply shrugged Sunflower off with an unconvincing reply, "You may be right. Thanks for your help."

Sunni put the phone down. The news of Dalan's suicide was disturbing. Dalan had been in charge of extracurricular activities at the university they both attended. She had spent several weekends teaching Sunni how to waltz. Sunni remembered those days twirling around the university gymnasium with great fondness. They had laughed uproariously every time they inadvertently stepped on each other's toes. When Sunni left China, Dalan's son had already turned two. Dalan and her husband still seemed very much in love and satisfied with their lives. People thought of them as a good match.

A decade later, Dalan's teenaged boy was motherless. Sunni was lost in these thoughts when she trudged out of the bathroom and sat down at the table beside Ida.

"Mommy, look at this!" Ida exclaimed gleefully, turning to see her mother's reaction to the tree she had shaped out of Rice Krispies. "Can I wake up Daddy now?" she cajoled.

Sunni reached out to her, pulling her close. "Who do you love? Mommy or Daddy?"

"Both."

"Who do you love more?"

"Sometimes, Mommy. Sometimes, Daddy." Ida caressed Sunni's face. "Why are you crying, Mommy?"

"One of Mommy's old friends is dead."

"Why? Can't a doctor cure the dead?"

"No, no, they can't."

"Was your friend very old?"

"Yes," Sunni replied, knowing that she should not try to talk about Dalan's suicide with her daughter.

"Mommy, when are we going to the movie?" Ida asked, slipping off her lap and running toward the front door where their coats hung on hooks.

"Soon," Sunni replied, composing herself. "Can you play for a couple of minutes by yourself?"

Sunni returned to the bathroom to splash some cold water on her face. The running water sounded to her like someone weeping. Even when she thought she had turned the faucet off, the water continued to drip like blood being shed into the sink.

Sunni felt exactly the desperation Dalan must have experienced in order to blindly slice at her skin, the blood rushing out like a relief of sorts. She could picture Dalan's son. The boy was crying out, "Please! I want my mom back!"

Sunni blinked her eyes rapidly in an attempt to erase the image from her mind. She made her way to the kitchen where she drank some juice, and her tightened throat finally relaxed.

She sat motionless for a moment, clutching her glass. Then she decided to check on Paul in the bedroom.

He was still sleeping like a baby. She felt her hand clench into a fist and she realized that all she wanted was to hit him. When her fist almost reached his head, she opened her palm instead, moving it like a small piece of cloth over his eyes. His head tilting away, Paul muttered, "No … no. Go away."

"Get up. It's nearly ten."

"I need more sleep," he said, removing Sunni's hand from his forehead and turning to face the wall.

"Ida's waiting for us to take her to the IMAX," Sunni insisted.

"Why don't you go by yourselves? … I'm tired," he said, pulling the blanket over his head.

"Damn you!" she hissed, her hand pressing against his shoulder, wanting it to hurt him, knowing it was a futile gesture.

Sunni and Ida left the apartment building and joined the crowds on the bustling street. They hopped onto a bus, transferred to the subway, and finally reached Le Vieux-Port. Ida's excitement was palpable.

They entered the cinema and found their seats. The movie was about a European boy coming by boat to find his grandmother in New York. With one hand, Ida held onto a bag of popcorn, while she stretched the other toward the waves crashing around the ship on the screen. It felt as though the waves were hurtling toward them, threatening to swallow them whole. Even Sunni was mesmerized by the rushing water. She blinked rapidly, as though she could avoid the current pulling her first toward land, and then inextricably out to sea. Suddenly, she thought she spotted Crazy Wen climbing out of the water, walking purposely toward her, a childhood nightmare coming back to haunt her.

**

In Sunni's dreams, half of Crazy Wen's head rose out of the water as the waves rolled to shore, spent and serene. Five-year-old Sunni gazed at that half-face and imagined Crazy Wen sucking air into his lungs as he swam, so that she felt less terrified. But suddenly, Wen's head floated toward her, bubbles popping from his mouth that seemed to shout, "Don't be afraid. I'm not … not crazy."

"Are you … are you still alive?" Sunni stammered.

"Ha! I died a while ago." His mouth spouted a cluster of bubbles.

"But, you're speaking," she whispered.

"Why not? Haven't you heard the story of Liang and Zhu?"

"Yes. My grandma told me they turned into butterflies." Thinking about the story suddenly erased her fears. "Are you going to turn into a butterfly?"

"Into a butterfly? That's a nice story, but I'm a ghost now."

"There're no ghosts in the world. You lie!"

"Look out! What's that?"

Sunni managed to open her eyes, but saw nothing. The body in the water had vanished, and Elephant Trunk Hill no longer existed. Crazy Wen's huge head gradually drifted across the sky, his long hair fluttering with the wind. His mouth was a large black hole with a half-red and half-white tongue stretching toward Sunni.

"Mom! Grandma!" Sunni screamed and fled. Lightning flashed, and she kicked off her quilt.

"Wake up! Wake up Sunni!" Her grandmother rushed into her room and pulled Sunni into her arms, gently rocking her back to sleep.

"I'm scared…," Sunni said, slowly drifting off to sleep.

"Shhhh, it's nothing, just a dream," said her grandmother, as she slipped Sunni back under the covers and pulled the quilt over her shoulders.

She tiptoed out of the room, but no sooner had she closed the door that Sunni shouted out again, "Crazy … Crazy Wen!" This time, she bolted upright and clutched the quilt with both hands, her face wet with sweat and tears.

Her grandmother returned and switched on the light. "I'm here. Sweetie, you'll be okay," she said, wiping Sunni's face with a handkerchief from the night table.

"I dreamed of Crazy Wen, who was really scary," Sunni said, her shoulders still quaking with fear.

"You shouldn't have gone to see Crazy Wen's body in the water," her grandmother chided.

"I promise not to go see the dead anymore."

"I'll stay here with you until you fall asleep," Sunni's grandmother said, climbing in beside her, and pulling the quilt up over both their shoulders. In a few minutes, she was snoring softly, but Sunni did not fall asleep again until just before dawn.

***

"Mommy!" Ida pulled Sunni's blouse. "That boy has found his grandma!"

"Oh?" Sunni said, startled into the present. The screen displayed a scene of the boy with his grandmother's family in New York. They were standing together, posing for a photograph.

After the movie, Sunni took Ida to her favourite McDonald's, where she could get a free toy with her meal. As Ida followed Sunni out of the restaurant, skipping happily along the sidewalk, she embraced her new little toy figure – a prince who matched the princess she had gotten on an earlier visit. It was obvious that Ida had enjoyed their Saturday outing, during which Sunni had finally arrived at a solution.

When they reached home, Paul was on his way out.

"Daddy! Look, I got a toy prince!" Ida exclaimed.

"Good. That's good, honey," Paul said distractedly, patting Ida's shoulder.

"Do you have a minute?" Sunni asked Paul as she led her daughter into the apartment. "Ida, do you want to play with your new prince?"

"Yes." Ida said, clapping her hands as she ran into the living room.

"Sunni, I left you a note on the dresser," said Paul, his eyes not able to meet hers.

Paul followed Sunni into the bedroom. She grabbed the note and read, "Sunni, I've thought this over carefully and I've decided to leave home for a while. If you can be rational, I can tell you the truth…."

"Tell me now," Sunni's voice sounded calm as she forced him to meet her steely gaze.

Paul closed the bedroom door. He looked at Sunni with caution. "My ex-girlfriend wants me back. We've been seeing each other for a while now. I … I don't think I can stop seeing her, Sunni."

"So all this time you've been lying to me about coming home late, night after night?" Sunni quivered, her cheeks flushed with shame and anger.

"I didn't have any other way –"

"What do you mean there was no other way? What about the truth? You say she came back? Why did she leave you in the first place?"

"She wanted me to give up my Ph.D. studies and travel with her to South America. I didn't agree so she got mad and left me."

"When did that happen?"

"The same year I met you. She was very immature at that time…"

"Now you are the one who is immature. You used me to replace her." Sunni raised her voice. "Paul! You are not the man I thought you were. Just leave. I don't think I want to ever see you again."

"You can have anything you want, Sunni. And I promise to pay child support for Ida." He drew a breath and added, "You've given me a lot these years. I feel guilty about leaving you and Ida, but I feel I don't have any choice."

"You leave me no choice, either," she said evenly as Paul trudged out of the bedroom. "You can go now," she added, pointing to the door.

Paul didn't respond. When he passed the living room, he hesitated but didn't stop. Picking up his briefcase from the couch, he pulled open the door, and stepped out of their lives.

Sunni sat on the bed and quietly sobbed. Ida heard her and raced into the room with her toys. "Mommy, please don't cry. I'll play with you." Ida's hands gently caressed Sunni's face. "You can have the prince *and* the princess, Mommy."

Sunni composed herself for Ida's sake. Rising to her feet, she took Ida's hands in her own. "Don't worry, Ida. Mommy won't cry anymore." Taking several deep breaths, Sunni felt her heart pump with new energy. Her attention was suddenly drawn to the wall calendar hanging in the living room. Two butterflies with black spots on their creamy-coloured wings seemed to drift from out of her head and land delicately on the calendar's glossy paper, becoming part of the scenic garden printed there. Sunni felt suddenly more awake than she had in a very long time. She knew that once she turned the page on the calendar, the image it displayed would be more real, and more beautiful than anything her memory might conjure from the past.

"Let's go Ida," she said purposely, "We have much to do today."

WILD ONIONS

SHA WAS ASSIGNED TO Red Rock Middle School as a seventh grader and moved into the dormitory in September of 1966. The school was located in Red Rock, a small town ten kilometres from her home in Chongqing City.

After Sha and other new students deposited their luggage in their allotted dormitory rooms, a Red Guard, a girl of about sixteen, showed them around the campus. Noticing only empty classrooms, Sha was puzzled. "Where are the students and teachers?"

The Red Guard patted her shoulder and chuckled. "Do you know anything about the Cultural Revolution?"

Sha nodded, remembering that teachers were under heavy criticism, and thus not allowed to teach; and then she shook her head, wondering why students were enrolled in the school if there were no classes.

The Red Guard pointed at the posters on the wall that were crowded with large-sized Chinese characters hand-painted with an ink brush: "Look! As students this is what we do: We follow Chairman Mao's instructions and criticize, and denounce, the feudalism, capitalism, and revisionism that was taught and spread in the schools before the Cultural Revolution."

"How do we do this?" asked another new student.

"Read all the posters around the school; join in the Red Guards' activities, and bring Maoism to every corner of the world." The Red Guard waved her hand through the air as if she were literally spreading

Maoism into every corner of the dormitory.

"Can we join the Red Guards?"

"No. We don't accept anybody under fourteen. In addition, only students who are the children of workers, poor peasants, and/or revolutionary cadres are qualified to be Red Guards."

Sha's heart skipped a beat. Her parents did not belong to any of those groups, and besides, she was not even thirteen years old.

"But," the Red Guard added, "you can come to help us. Our office is Room 109 in the administration building."

The following day, Sha made her way to Room 109. Like some of the other students, she copied the critical articles written by some of the Red Guards on large-sized paper with an ink brush. The students were told to make a few copies of each article and then post them in different locations, on and off campus. After a few weeks, Sha was pleased to find that her brush writing skills had improved considerably. Also, she dutifully read through the contents of all the large-character posters.

Sha shared a huge room with twelve other girls. Some of her roommates were Red Guards. They asked Sha and the other girls to join them for the Loyalty Dance. To demonstrate their loyalty to Chairman Mao, the girls danced holding a red, heart-shaped piece of cardboard with the Chinese character for "loyalty" brushed on with gold paint. Sha practiced the dance with a group of girls who called themselves the Maoist Propaganda Team. Sometimes, they performed the dance on the village streets.

In the evening Sha did not have any assignments to complete since the students had no classes to attend. Most literary works had been banned, and most movies had been labelled "poisonous weeds." The cinema was used to criticize or denounce eight kinds of enemies defined by the revolutionary masses: landowners, the rich, anti-revolutionaries, evils, rightists, traitors, spies, and capitalists.

In Sha's room, the girls told each other stories to kill time. Whether sacred or ghostly, real or fictive, storytelling became an overwhelming preoccupation.

One evening, the girls climbed into their beds at the usual hour. As soon as one of the roommates said, "Turn off the light," Sha pulled her quilt over her head to shield herself from the dark. However, her desire to listen to a new story was so strong that she poked her head out from under the quilt, straining to hear a voice. The room was so dim that for a moment she could not see anything. *The door's closed,* she told herself. *Don't be scared.*

"On a starless night, in this hall," the hoarse voice of a storyteller blew like a gust of wind against her face. "A student named Ling dreamt of a long-haired girl in a white robe who patted her shoulders, and said, 'Wake up! Time for reading.' Ling suddenly opened her eyes, but no one was there."

"What happened next?" asked Sha, eyes wide, her quilt wrapped tightly around her.

"Listen," the storyteller said, clapping her hands for silence. "Since Ling had the same dream over and over, she told her dream to others. Finally, the story of the dream reached Nanny Wang in the kitchen. And guess what she said?"

"What did Nanny Wang say?" asked all the girls in the room at the same time as if they were reciting one of Chairman Mao's quotations.

"She said, 'Don't be afraid. The girl in the white robe is the spirit of the merciful old nun. She used to read prayers in that room.'"

"What? The old nun!"

"Yeah. Nanny Wang said the old nun hanged herself in this hall in 1949 after the Communists' takeover."

"Is it possible? There are no such things as ghosts," whispered one girl.

"The soul isn't a ghost. The souls of good people never disappear," replied another girl with certainty.

Until midnight, the girls in Sha's room exchanged opinions about the existence of souls and ghosts.

Sometimes at midnight a loudspeaker would rouse them from their sleep, and announce Mao's latest political statement broadcast by radio. When this happened, the students would knock on each door in the dormitory, calling out, "Get up! Let's celebrate!" Sha would dress quickly and follow the other students out, each holding onto Mao's red book. The Red Guards would make sure to sport red armbands.

The leading group would play drums, beat bronze gongs and cymbals. Some would hold national flags. Sha would walk among the excited celebrators streaming down the narrow streets of Red Rock with their arms raised, shouting, "Long live Chairman Mao!" and "Follow Chairman Mao forever!" Sha would join the others, prancing and singing songs. Often, she would take notice of several of the town's residents standing under streetlights, watching the melee, yawning, or rubbing their eyes with handkerchiefs.

***

Another morning, Sha followed some of her roommates to the street to watch different groups of Red Guards argue with one another.

Among the crowd gathering in front of a three-storey government building in the town centre, a male student, about fifteen years old, waved his arms in the air, the scarlet band on his arm and its gold characters, "Red Guard," glistening in the sun. He shouted, "We're the best revolutionary team in town. Don't you agree?"

"Yes! We are!" Several students raised their arms.

"No, you're not!" A girl pushed through the crowd toward the boy. "We denounced the school principal at our meeting last Friday. Why didn't your team join us?"

"We went to the municipal meeting to denounce the mayor," yelled another girl, who held up both her arms.

"We've already criticized the principal. Now we're going to knock down a big capitalist lackey. Do you understand?" The boy laughed and shook some sheets of paper in his hand. When he let go of them, the flyers fluttered over the crowd. "Comrades, read our political statement!" His voice echoed in front of the wall of the building covered by large-character posters.

Sha caught one and read it.

"Look who's here." Someone tugged at her blouse.

Sha spun around and saw her roommate, Lilei, with a girl about eleven years old. It was the sister of Sha's friend. "Fang! Why did you come into town?" asked Sha with surprise.

"Do you know where my sister has gone? Nobody seems to know anything about her," said the girl, with a confused look on her face.

"She's gone to the revolutionary holy place, Yan'an," Sha answered.

"What?" Fang didn't expect this answer. "She went to Yan'an! That's so far away," she said, her eyes wide with fear.

"Don't worry, Fang." Sha explained that many students wanted to follow in the steps of Mao who had led the Red Army on a Long March on foot for two years – from 1934-1936 – during the battle with Chiang Kai-shek's Nationalist Party. "Your sister joined a Long March team and left last week."

"Do you know when they will get there?"

"I'm not sure. Maybe in a month or two."

"My parents don't know she's gone." Fang wiped her sweaty face with a handkerchief. "She hasn't been home for three weeks. That's why I came to find her."

"How did you get here?"

"On foot! The bus drivers stopped working because they are on revolutionary duties."

"Come with me to my dorm." Sha gripped Fang's hand and left the crowd. "Your sister asked me to tell your parents about her Long March when I went home. But I was too busy to leave last weekend."

"My mom says you don't have any classes. So what are you doing in school?"

"Reading wall posters, shouting 'Defend Chairman Mao' and 'Down with Liu Shaoqi' at the denunciation meetings. We also join in street demonstrations, like the one you saw just now." Sha pointed to a building. "Look, this is my dorm."

"It looks like a temple."

"It'd been a convent until it became a student dorm seventeen years ago."

Sha led Fang through the courtyard. They went upstairs and entered Sha's room.

"Why are many of the beds empty?" asked Fang.

"Some students like your sister are away on their Long March." Sha shook her head. "Some may fear the revolution and hide at home."

"Now I understand why you don't go home."

"What do you mean?" asked Sha.

"You want to make revolution."

"Most of my roommates are eighth graders or older," Sha explained enthusiastically. "Some of them are Red Guards. They are from Red

Rock, but they don't go home."

"You must like it here. But I want to stay home."

"We're not here for fun. Some girls' homes are just a five-minute walk away from here, but they live in the dorm to participate in revolutionary activities. Do you remember the girl who brought you to me, Lilei? Her dad is the school principal and a capitalist lackey. This is why she moved into the school – to show her loyalty to the revolution. I like these girls and want to learn from them," Sha said as she retrieved a box from her drawer and opened it. "Have some cookies. I'll find water for you."

She checked a few thermoses in the room for drinking water, but could only find a half glass of boiled water. Sha handed Fang the water and then pointed to her upper bunk bed.

"You can take a nap in my bed if you want," Sha said.

Fang nodded and climbed onto the bed.

***

"Wake up." Sha shook Fang's arm after she had read a few pages of Mao's red book and made some notes.

"What time is it?"

"Maybe four o'clock. Do you want to go pick wild onions?"

"Why?"

"The meals in the cafeteria are awful. We call them pigfeed."

"Pigfeed? Why?"

"Sometimes the rice is half cooked and the carrots and Chinese cabbage are mushy."

"My dad says we should live a simple life to fight against bourgeois ideas. But I don't think I would like pigfeed."

"It tastes salty and watery. But I can make a salad with wild onions and chilli peppers."

"Sounds good. Let's go." Fang came down from the top bunk.

Sha and Fang walked into a field near the school. The sunlight beamed through the gaps between the hills and coloured the late autumn. Stones shone among yellow grass, and golden brown leaves hung from the almost bare trees. Faded white and yellow flowers, and red and black wild-berries, dotted the bushes. Weeds waved among a jumble of rocks, and fallen leaves danced with the wind.

Sha enjoyed the quiet wilderness. All the wall posters, red slogans, denunciation meetings, and busy crowds that filled her mind disappeared. Suddenly, she felt lonely and homesick. Dad's thoughtful eyes under his glasses, Mom's over-elaborate words, and her younger sister's playhouse made of little stools, came alive in her memory.

Thinking about her family, Sha sighed. *Chairman Mao asks us to participate in the revolution. But I don't have the right family background to become a Red Guard.* She shivered, and tried to push thoughts of her mother's background out of her mind.

Once she asked her mother, "Do I have grandparents?"

"Yes, but they are dead."

"How?"

"They just died." Her mother was reluctant to talk about them.

Later, after reading a note in her family's residence booklet, Sha discovered that her mother had been born to a landowner's family. Since she was a little girl, Sha had been told at school that all landowners had exploited the working class. As a result, landowners were classified as sinners and enemies of the revolution. She felt guilty about her grandparents, but felt glad that the class enemies on her maternal family's side had vanished from the world.

After spotting a tall wild onion, Sha stepped forward and bent to pull it out. A pungent scent drifted into her nostrils. Dropping to her knees, she pushed away the weeds to get at the large wild onion heads. Unexpectedly, her head bumped into something hard. She looked up and discovered a cracked gravestone. It lay alone among the rocks, framed by a mass of tangled weeds. The inscription on the stone was blurry though she could still recognize a few words: "A devoted woman … under the Nine … Friends…" The date was not legible. A wooden board had been inserted into the grave, and a few words scribbled with red paint read: "The nun deserves death!" Sha's heart sank, knowing that the Red Guards had been there to denounce the nun who had died seventeen years before. She stared at the headstone for a while. Chills ran through her body.

Sha touched Mao's badge on the front of her sweater and desperately wondered: *Who will have this badge if I die? If I die, where will I go? Where am I? Why am I here?* She felt as if her body had become airy and weightless. Everything that had seemed extraordinarily clear was now vague and uncertain. Her thoughts flew far away into an invisible world, and she felt helpless and terrified. Sitting on the ground, almost bursting into tears, she finally shrieked, "Fang!"

"Yeah? I'm here!" Fang ran up to her. "An old tomb! Maybe it's empty. Do you think ghosts exist?"

Staring at Fang, Sha shook her head.

Fang pulled Sha to her feet. "Let's go home. I'm starving."

"Okay. We have enough onions for supper."

The two girls walked away from the wilderness, their shadows lengthening behind them as the sun went down.

**

A month later, Sha joined a group of teenaged students who had decided to follow Mao's instruction that bourgeois youth must receive re-education from the working class. Most of the students that needed more re-education came from the families of doctors, teachers, lawyers, scientists, and researchers – all intellectuals were labelled "Stinking Number Nines" because they were ranked after the other eight identified types of "evil people." Laden with their luggage, the group trudged along to a factory, fifteen kilometres away from the school. In the factory, the students were directed to help the cooks in the kitchen.

"You girls, wash these vegetables." One of the cooks cut off the roots of napa, Chinese cabbages, and soaked them in a huge sink.

Sha and two other girls donned aprons and bent over to rinse the huge pile of napa. Sha's fingers deftly moved along the leaves in the water. She was a little disappointed as she did not get the chance to learn how to operate a machine or how to produce goods in the factory. She had not expected to end up working in the kitchen.

One of the boys beside her asked another cook, "We have strength. Can we knead the dough?"

"Sure. Watch me first." The cook turned over a large basin, dumping a large mound of dough onto the board. He took a kitchen knife and cut the dough into a couple of pieces. "Take one. Roll it out with your hands like this." The cook demonstrated. "Got it?" The boys rolled up their sleeves.

Sha became accustomed to her chores in the kitchen, and time dragged on. She wondered how long this type of revolutionary life would last.

Two weeks passed. One evening, a fellow student who had left in the early morning to find out what was going on in school, returned with shocking news. "The Defending East Long March Team has returned. They carried back a student with a leg fracture after he fell from a truck. The June 11th Fighting Team got marked as an anti-Mao organization, and —" he hesitated for an instant then said, "I've heard that Principal Yu committed suicide by ingesting poison as he couldn't bear the denunciation."

Sha turned around to search for Lilei and found her squatting with both hands on her face, tears streaming down her face.

"This is your mail," the same student called to Sha.

She did not have time to comfort Lilei. She took the crumpled letter. It had her father's handwriting on it. With shaking hands, she opened the letter. It read:

Nov. 14, 1966
Dear Sha,
Your mother is very ill. She was hospitalized yesterday. The doctor said she needs surgery. Hope you can return home as soon as pos-sible.
Your father

The letter had been mailed two weeks earlier.

Lilei, silently weeping over her father's death, and Sha, her face clouded with fear and worry, dragged themselves back to the school that same evening.

Again, there were no buses. The following morning, Sha walked home. It took her over two hours to get there.

She pushed the door open and saw the nanny sitting with her sister. "Nanny Li, is my dad home?"

"Oh, dear. You're back." The elderly woman wiped her eyes.

"How's my mom?"

"She … she couldn't wait. She is gone."

"No, no, she is not!" Sha's mouth twitched. She grasped the woman's hand as she sobbed. "Where is my dad?"

"He'll be back soon. Sit down, poor thing." Nanny Li patted Sha on the back and sighed. "Good people live short lives. You don't know how much your mother worried about you. You shouldn't have lived at school."

"I needed to join in the Cultural Revolution," Sha explained in tears.

"I don't know why we need a revolution." Shaking her head, Nanny Li wheezed. "Poor girl, you're more confused than me."

Sha sat on a chair, sobbing. Her six-year-old sister did not understand what had happened, but she walked over to Sha and cried along with her. Sha clasped the little girl in her arms. The solitary tomb in the field reappeared in front of her. The missing words inscribed on the cracked gravestone became clear: "A devoted religious woman of the world, whose soul now rests beneath the Nine Springs; a place for the dead."

***

It was some time afterward that Sha discovered a worn envelope in a suitcase left by her mother. Inside was a faded photograph of her mother when she was about fifteen years old. On the back it read, "Shuzhen Feng from Yude Girls' School, Chongqing, July 1945." She also found a small metal cross with a figure of Jesus on it. Her first interpretation was: Mom was superstitious. She did not ask her father about the photograph and cross because she knew no answers would be forthcoming. Her parents had never mentioned her mother's past since her mother's family had been labelled "evil." Sha carefully hid the photo in a safe place. The next evening, she dug a hole under a tree outside the apartment building. Looking around and seeing nobody, she laid the cross into the hole and covered it with dirt. The snow fell and whitened the spot immediately.

***

Years later, Sha became a Ph.D. student at the University of Toronto, Canada. In the summer of 1986, she spent hours in the university archives daily, doing research for her dissertation on the women missionaries from the United Church, who had worked in Sichuan Province, China. Sha flipped through piles of The Annual Reports of the Women's Missionary Society of the Methodist/United Church of Canada month by month. Suddenly, a photo with the heading, "1945 Graduation Class of Yude Girls' School" caught her eye. With eagerness, she read the accompanying article.

The author, Margaret Bliss, detailed her missionary experience with Yude Girls' School in the 1940s. According to Margaret's tale, Honglin Feng, the richest landowner in the Nanshan area, was converted to Christianity. Then he became the first parent to send his daughter, Shuzhen, to the girls' school. Following his example, five other families allowed their daughters to attend the same school.

A class photo that accompanied the essay rang a bell. *Is this photo the one I found twenty years ago?* She wondered as she examined the young faces and recognized her mother among them. Margaret Bliss's story helped uncover the mystery of her mother's family. Sha finally understood why her mother had that graduation photo and metal cross as keepsakes. She felt proud of her mother and sorrow for her confused youth during the Cultural Revolution.

Returning the copy of the missionary monthly to the service desk, she asked for Margaret Bliss's address.

The archivist located the information and said, "Margaret Bliss never married and doesn't have any immediate family members. In 1983 she moved into a nursing home in Montreal."

Sha thanked the archivist and copied down the address hoping that Margaret would remember her mother and could tell Sha more about her mother's past.

Back in her apartment, she wrote to Margaret Bliss asking to meet with her and mailed the letter.

She checked her mailbox everyday after that. Nine days later, her letter returned with a notice attached to the envelope: "Deceased."

***

At the end of August, Sha rode a train to Montreal. From the train station she got on a bus that took her out to a cemetery in the suburbs. The gate had a board on which the words, "The United Church," were carved. Sha wanted to pay respect to the woman who had taught and influenced her mother.

The lawn was bright green and birds twittered in the trees. Colourful flowers or wreaths were placed in front of the many crosses and headstones in the cemetery. Sha examined the words on each headstone as she strolled. The breeze blew the scent of freshly cut grass. With a deep breath, she seemed back in the open field where she had come across that ancient tomb. Sha envisioned her own little figure in the wild twenty years earlier.

At last, she located Margaret Bliss's grave. She laid a bunch of red roses by Margaret's headstone. Her words on a white ribbon read: "To Margaret Bliss, teacher of Shuzhen Feng. From Feng's daughter, Sha." She read the inscription on the stone again:

Margaret Bliss
Born on May 2, 1904
Back in the Lord's Hands on June 23, 1986
In Chongqing City of China, 1930-1952, for the Lord

She stood motionless. The broken tombstone in the field near Red Rock Middle School reappeared in front of her. She wondered if the nun's damaged tombstone had been repaired after the Cultural Revolution ended. The tiny cross buried in the memory of her childhood glittered in the sunlight. Suddenly, the aroma of wild onions wafted into her nostrils.

YEARNING

⁂

LIKE A THICK CURTAIN, the dusk concealed the quiet fields of the military farm near Jihong County, Yunnan Province, China. The hot air of an August evening clung to the barb-wired fields. Rusted iron posts stood alongside the trees and bushes, outlining a path that sprawled to the faraway woods. Under a massive fir tree, a young man and woman, both about twenty years old, silently stood.

"Nina, why don't you say something?"

The girl bit her lip. "What else can I say?" She jerked her head upward, looking him in the eyes. "Hai, do you love me?"

"Yes, but I can't go with you." Hai's hand fanned mosquitoes away from Nina's face. "Love isn't everything. I must go to Vietnam. I don't think it's right to sneak across the border to Hong Kong."

"You have to sneak across the border to Vietnam, too." Nina grasped Hai's hand. "But I wouldn't join the Vietcong. Think twice. I'm afraid you'll regret it."

"I want to be recognized as a revolutionary," said Hai. "It's that simple."

"And I can't live under the repression of the Cultural Revolution anymore. The land across the Pacific Ocean means freedom to me," said Nina, her hands on his chest, her eyes imploring him to change his mind.

"Maybe both of us are wrong. Who knows?" Hai's eyes locked with Nina's, and a twinge of sadness pierced his heart. Pulling Nina gently toward him, he embraced her. "I'm sorry to have kept you waiting. I've thought it over and I can't follow the path my parents took before me. They're enemies of the Communist Party, but I believe in communism. It's wrong to say that 'a hero father raises a revolutionary son, and a reactionary father raises an anti-revolutionary bastard.' Even though my parents are anti-revolutionaries, I am not. I need to prove that I'm a revolutionary, and the only way I can do this is to join the Vietcong in an anti-American war."

"You're so headstrong." Nina quavered and withdrew herself from his arms. "What's the use of proving yourself different from your parents? Nobody treats us like human beings because of our family backgrounds. Since the Cultural Revolution, we have simply been branded as evil." She shook her shorthaired head. "We've tried hard to remould ourselves here. But because of our family backgrounds, we will always be second-class citizens. I'd rather take my chances someplace where I can be free."

"Right, take your chances." Hai nodded. "In case …"

"In case what?" Nina stared into his brown eyes.

"If I die, tell my brother and sister my story if you ever see them again."

"If I die, go find my mother, but don't say a word about me," said Nina, irritated.

"Enough, let's stop." Hai hesitated, but reached out his arms again to draw Nina close. At the prospect of leaving her, his heart sank into a dark well, but he could not relinquish his plan to go to Vietnam—his only chance to prove himself.

Nina clenched her fists and punched his chest. "I'll blame you forever," she sobbed, unable to speak anymore.

Hai held Nina tighter to him. "Forgive me. But we both need to do what we must."

She stopped weeping. With her hand over his mouth, she cried out, "We deserve a better life. Something's wrong with this society, not us. I'll regret it if I don't try to escape and I'm sorry that you aren't coming with me. I fear you are making a mistake." Leaning her head against his chest, Nina was calmed by the beating of his heart against her ear.

A gust of wind wrapped itself around their bodies and they shivered under the darkening sky. The sound of a dog's barking brought the reality of their future steps closer. Nina remembered she had a meeting with her girlfriend, Dew, to plan for the next day's trip to Kunming. She whispered to Hai with sudden urgency, "I've got to go."

"You go." Hai clasped her head with his palms, and his lips covered hers. A favourite phrase of his mother occurred to him, and despite his aversion to it, he repeated it now. "God bless you."

Nina pulled herself away from him with a muffled "Goodbye." She hurried away toward the end of the path. When she turned her head, she could just barely distinguish his lanky figure; it looked as if it were engulfed in the darkness.

Watching Nina fade away, Hai almost called out, "Wait! I'll come with you." He felt frozen, heartbroken. That he might never see her again in his life was a tangible reality. He covered his eyes with his hands, but could not stop the tears, and they dripped through his fingers. Like a puppet on strings, he shambled back to the hut he shared with twelve other young farm workers.

***

Before lunchtime the following day, Nina gripped a telegram sent by her cousin, Ray, in Guangzhou, and rushed into the head office of the military farm. A middle-aged man sat at a desk, his greying head bent over a newspaper.

"Chairman Yang, may I ask for a personal leave since it's not the busy season now?"

Yang craned his head away from the paper in his hands. Noticing her puffy eyelids and red-rimmed eyes, he asked, "Nina, what's wrong?"

"My mother's been hospitalized." Nina handed her telegram to him. "Look at this."

"'Return home. Mother's sick.'" Yang read it aloud, scrutinizing the date. "Why don't you talk to Commissar Zhao?"

"I did, Sir. He said I needed your permission for a two-week leave, or longer."

"Well, it looks like you haven't been home since you came here last year." Yang looked as if he had something to mull over. Nina prayed that he would not reject her request. She could hardly breathe until he finally agreed. "Okay, but you must be back in three weeks."

"Thank you so much." Nina was surprised to find that her hands were trembling.

"Being away from the farm doesn't mean you can stop reforming your thoughts. Mind your P's and Q's and follow Mao's instructions every day. Can you remember that?"

"Yes, Chairman Yang." Nina left the office and hurried back to the dormitory while her roommates still worked in the cornfields.

Nina packed her belongings hastily and left the compound before anyone returned from the fields. She carried a worn green canvas handbag over her left shoulder and gripped the handles of a dark blue travel bag with her right hand as she trudged along the road toward Simao County. She narrowed her eyes to shield them from the stark midday sun. The green crops looked like huge rugs blanketing the fields. A profound sadness filled her chest when she thought about Hai. But she did not turn her head; she was afraid she would lose the courage. She could hear herself screaming from the bottom of her heart, "Farewell!"

Nina had walked for about ten minutes when she heard horseshoes tapping behind her. Dew arrived in a horse-drawn wagon just as expected.

"Get in," said Dew, as she guided the horse to a stop. She reached down to take Nina's bags and then pulled her up over the side of the wagon.

Nina dropped onto the hard seat. Free from the tension in her shoulders, the exhaustion of a sleepless night fell over her like a darkened tent. The rocking motion of the wagon and clopping rhythm of the horseshoes helped her drift off to sleep.

After a few hours of restless slumber, she finally opened her eyes. Night had fallen. There was no moon, only the silvery light of a star-filled sky. The horse's snorting reminded her she was in a wagon that had stopped at the roadside.

"Dew?"

"We're close to Kunming," said Dew as she handed her an open canister. "Here's something to eat. I've just had something, too."

"Thanks." Nina grabbed a steamed bun from the canister. Her growling stomach betrayed her hunger. She wasn't satisfied until she had gobbled down three buns. After quaffing water from a canteen, she asked, "Do you think your boyfriend will be on duty on today's train?"

"I'm not sure," Dew said with a shrug, her bobbed hair springing lightly off her shoulders. "His schedule changes all the time, and you are a couple of days late. I had no way to reach him and let him know you were still coming."

"I'm sorry, Dew," said Nina, holding back the tears that unexpectedly clouded her eyes. She had waited to leave, hoping that Hai would change his mind. She couldn't explain all this to her friend. There wasn't time. "What do you think I should do? Should I try to find him?"

"Get on the train by yourself at first. Only try to find him if you get caught without a ticket."

"Okay, I'll take my chances." Nina grasped Dew's hand. "I really appreciate your help and will repay you in the future."

"Don't mention it," Dew said, smiling. "Our moms are old friends so I think of you as my sister. I am glad to help, and I wish you the best."

The horse-drawn wagon resumed its way toward Western Hill Station. The feeling of leaving her friends forever and facing an uncertain future came flooding back to Nina. She wept like a little girl under night's curtain.

Finally, Dew parked the wagon near the station in Kunming where a lonesome train whistle broke the quiet of dawn. Nina climbed out of the cart. She rummaged through her handbag and pulled out a package covered in brown paper, which she then placed in Dew's hand. She had been saving this gift for Dew for a long time, having purchased it months before from a friend who had smuggled some prohibited items into the compound. "This is for you; a silk scarf, to remember me by. Be careful on your way back."

Dew held back her tears and hugged the package to her chest. "Don't worry about me. You take care."

Nina patted Dew's hand reassuringly, although she herself felt uncertain and afraid. "Goodbye Dew, and thank you," she said, as she turned and spotted a side entrance to the station under a dim streetlamp where train workers came and went. She headed toward it. Through the station window she could see a man resting his head on a table, clearly asleep. Without hesitation, Nina scampered past the security booth where a whiff of cigarette smoke drifted from the small opening and mingled with the odour of diesel.

When she reached the barren platform, she used her travel bag as a stool, and waited.

The train arrived an hour later. When she boarded it, nobody asked to see her ticket. She could not find anywhere to sit and had to nudge the people in the aisle to reach the end of the car. Wading through car after car, she finally spotted an empty spot near an elderly and kind-looking woman. She squeezed in her luggage and plunked herself on top of it. By the time she settled, many passengers had awakened. Some stretched their arms or legs, and others stumbled across the crowded aisle toward a washroom or the dining car. Nina watched as a few crew members hurried past. She was determined not to ask about Dew's boyfriend unless she was in a real pinch.

About an hour later, a loudspeaker announced a ticket check, which required the passengers' co-operation. Nina stood up with her bags and walked hastily into a nearby washroom, locking the door securely behind her. In the stinking room, Nina reached her head up toward the half-ajar window for fresh air. As she waited, she could hear people shuffling, questioning, and arguing. The jumble of noise lasted about fifteen minutes and then receded. Relieved, she left the washroom and returned to her spot.

"I thought you'd gotten a seat somewhere else." The elderly woman looked up at her, drawing back her legs to leave Nina some space.

"Thank you. I went to the washroom. I have a terrible stomach ache." She could not reveal the real reason behind her retreat to the washroom.

"A lad got fined fifty yuan for not having a ticket. That's a lot of money."

Nina drew a breath. *My eight yuan would not have gotten me far.* At least she hadn't needed to call on Dew's boyfriend, and put him at risk, too.

***

Three days later, Nina slept soundly in a dust-layered room on Lujing Road in Guangzhou City.

In her dream, she was a child again, and her mother sat beside her in bed. Her mother's warm hand gently caressed Nina's hair. Before she could look directly into her mother's face, her childhood faded like a shred of cloud merging into the sky.

She opened her eyes to dust particles dancing in the afternoon sunshine that penetrated the window curtains. She heard a knock on the door and approached it with caution. "Who is it?" she asked.

Nina was relieved when she heard her eighteen-year-old cousin, Ray, answer. He pushed open the door and walked in. "Did you have a good sleep?"

"Yes."

"What time can we leave?"

"I … I…" Nina stammered. "I want to say goodbye to my mother, but am afraid of getting us into trouble."

"It's not a good idea," Ray said, raising his eyebrows and looking somewhat alarmed. "She might be charged with planning it. It's better if she knows nothing about it. If we fail, she will see us behind bars."

"You're right." Nina said, reaching for her clothes on the chair next to the bed. Ray turned his eyes away and squatted to arrange his items in the corner.

That evening, Nina and Ray paced back and forth on Yuexiu Street North, gazing up at a building across the street. When Nina finally noticed a blurred figure in the lit window, she drew a deep breath. "I've seen my mom. Let's get going."

"We should've left long ago," replied Ray.

***

By train, they arrived in Shenzhen where Ray paid his contact to get supplies for their getaway.

At night, with the help of a map, Nina and Ray reached Defence Road in Sha Tau Kok and hid in a ditch nearby. The shore in the distance was invisible in the thickening darkness, but they could hear waves slapping on the beach and smell sea-grass. Time passed at an excruciatingly slow pace, but still they dared not budge until the People's Liberation Army patrol team left.

Both Ray and Nina had a basketball in a string bag tied to their waists.

After crossing Defence Road, they scampered along the shore toward the reef, where they found a boat camouflaged with seaweed. Nina pulled away the seaweed and Ray cut the rope attached to the boat.

As they climbed into the boat, they noticed a blinking light in the sky.

"Be sure your wallet remains tied to your waist." Ray dipped two oars into the water. "How is your basketball? It will help you float when you're tired."

"They're both in the right place," answered Nina, sitting across from him at the other end of the boat. Her hands clasped the ball in front of her. Her voice quavered with fear. "What should I do?"

"Keep an eye open for anything suspicious." Ray propelled the boat smoothly and glided toward the east.

The sky darkened, and the oars creaked occasionally. The sounds of a distant engine soared over the water, and Nina could feel her heart pounding then slow down as she regained control of her edgy nerves.

About twenty minutes later, they could see the faintly-lit sky over the New Territories of Hong Kong.

Suddenly, an engine rumbled from the northeast. Nina's heart pounded as if it were about to jump into her mouth. "An army patrol boat is coming straight at us," she gasped. Ray's arms pulled the oars through the water as fast as they could muster.

The sound of the engine grew louder, indicating that a boat was speeding toward them. "What are we going to do?" asked Nina, panicked.

"Push the ball onto your back, drop into the water, and then swim east." Ray stopped rowing. "Hurry!" His voice was urgent.

Nina felt her body stiffen as she plopped into the water. She swallowed a mouthful of water and choked, but with Ray's voice echoing in her ears, she managed to propel her arms through the water in the direction he had pointed. Turning her head, she noticed Ray's boat moving in the opposite direction and heard the engine rattle away. Nina ploughed through the water until she touched several reeds.

Bang! Bang! Shots rose in the distance. She quailed and knelt into the sand. A chill spread through her limbs. She turned her head, her eyes wide open, but she could see nothing. The darkness blanketed the water and engulfed Ray's boat, as did the terrifying sound of the engine.

Wiping water off her face, Nina listened carefully, but heard nothing suspicious. She removed the netted basketball and plodded through the reeds. *Is Ray dead or alive?* The question flashed in her mind like lightning running across a darkened sky.

As she staggered to the grass-covered shore, it began raining. She waded through mud and bushes and darkness for what seemed like forever. Several scattered houses about fifty metres away loomed ahead of her, and she shuffled toward one of them. The rain was pouring heavily by the time she reached some kind of wall. Just as she was about to lean her weary body against it, a huge dog darted out from a corner and jumped on her.

"My God!" Nina's shriek held the dog back only momentarily; it flinched and then attacked her again. She stooped, groping at the ground with shivering hands. Before she could grab a rock, she felt the dog's teeth penetrate her leg. She screamed, hitting the dog's head with the stone at the same time.

The attacker yelped, then ran away, its tail drooping. Nina touched her leg and felt warm, sticky liquid mixing with the cool rain. Blood! She collapsed as if struck by a thunderbolt.

***

"Mom!" a child called out, "her eyes are moving!"

Nina slowly opened her eyes. A little boy was staring into her face. She could see that she was lying on a low bed in a strange room; she blinked hard, trying to remember what had happened.

"Don't be afraid," said a woman who looked to be in her thirties as she walked into the room with a bowl in her hand. "Did you slip through the border?"

Before Nina responded, the woman continued, "Last night I heard a dog barking, and then somebody shrieking. I rushed out and saw you lying on the ground."

Nina sat up, feeling some pain in her left leg. She lifted the sheet draped over her leg and saw a bandage wrapped tightly around her calf, which triggered the memory of the dog's assault. Looking up at the woman, Nina asked, "Did you bandage my leg?"

The woman nodded.

"Where am I?"

"Wu Kau Tang Village," answered the woman, as she sat on a chair by the bed.

"Is this your home?"

"Yes," said the woman. "Me and my hubby slipped from the Mainland in 1967. Now he's working on an oyster farm." She handed the bowl, with a spoon, to Nina. "You must be starving. Want some congee?"

Nina took the bowl gratefully. The warmth of the congee spread to her heart, which was still heavy with last night's nightmare. She burst into tears. *Where is Ray? How is Hai?*

"Don't weep." The woman patted her shoulder. "You'll feel better if you eat."

"Thank you for helping me," said Nina, wiping away her tears. "What should I call you?"

"Everybody calls me Gui's Wife or Gui's because my husband's family name is Gui. What's your name?"

"Nina."

"Strange name."

"It's Russian."

"You city people are always funny. Aren't you afraid of being called a 'running dog' since the Soviet Union is revisionist?"

"The Soviet Union was our fraternal country when my parents named me."

Nina spooned the congee into her mouth, devouring it as she had not eaten a home-cooked meal since she she had gone to live on the military farm. The pork congee tasted salty and sweet and was full of Chinese cabbage and lotus root.

Seeing Nina gulp the food, Gui's Wife asked with a chuckle, "Want another bowl?"

"Yes, please. It's delicious."

"Mom, I want a bowl of congee, too," said the boy.

"Go get it yourself, Bean." The mother smiled.

Nina felt better after she swallowed her second serving. No longer dizzy, she wanted to get out of bed. "Where're my jacket and pants?"

"Not dry yet. Try mine," said Gui's Wife as she pulled a blouse and a pair of slacks out of a closet.

"You are very kind," said Nina hugging the clothes to her chest. "Do you know how to get to the Office of Resident Affairs?"

"You'll have to ask Gui when he comes home. Don't worry; you'll get a resident card. Why don't you get dressed now and join me in the kitchen."

Nina took a few steps and was thankful that she was not in pain from the bite. She pulled on the baggy clothes and peered around the door. "Gui's, can I help you with anything?"

"My goodness!" Gui's Wife slapped her thigh, a broad grin on her face. "I forgot I was hanging kelp."

Nina followed Gui's Wife outdoors to a walled yard where half-dried kelp hung on bamboo sticks across a low wall, waving in the breeze that blew in salty air from the sea. Gui's Wife stooped over a vat to pick up kelp, piece by piece, and along with her, Nina hung the kelp on available bamboo sticks. The kelp swayed slightly. With a deep breath, Nina felt the sea again, and its familiar odour aroused more memories in her.

***

Five-year-old Nina enjoyed ambling on the beach with her mother, where she gathered seashells and colourful pebbles into the toy bucket she was carrying. As she spied sails in the choppy sea, she thought about her father, who was always busy, working on a naval base in Hainan, another province, and who only returned home once or twice a month. She wondered which one was her father's navy vessel and asked, "When will Daddy come home?"

"Perhaps in a week," answered her mother. "Someday we'll let you see what a navy vessel looks like."

"It must be big. Like that?" Little Nina tilted her head, and her arms stretched widely toward the far-away sails. The pail in her hand fell. The shells and pebbles fell onto the sand.

"Much bigger," answered her mother, with a wide smile. She helped refill Nina's pail. "You'll see."

Nina did not see her father often, let alone his vessel. She was ten when she finally got the opportunity to visit her father on the vessel along with her mother.

Nina climbed with her parents onto a warship anchored at a military port, which looked like a three-storey building floating over the water. Together they had a seafood meal in a light blue dining hall. Nina imagined the table would shake if the water pushed the ship, so she jumped hard on the floor, but nothing budged. After supper, the family strolled along a path in the military compound. Holding her mother's hand on one side and her father's on the other, Nina bounced along kicking up tiny rocks with joy. She raised her head to look at a number of dark green, basketball-sized objects in the high palm trees. "My heavens, what are those balls?"

Amused by her old-fashioned exclamation, her father laughed out loud. "Oh, my silly girl. They're coconuts."

"But I've never seen big coconuts like these." She pulled at her father's hand.

***

"Nina, take a break." Gui's Wife's loud voice dragged her back to the present. Turning around, Nina found the vat empty and all the kelp already on the sticks. Back in the living room, Gui's Wife brewed a pot of herbal tea.

"Are you hot?" asked Gui's Wife as she soaked the teapot in a basin of cold water. "In ten minutes, we'll drink cold tea. It's really good."

"You work very hard."

"I learned to do all kinds of chores as a little girl. Gui is more capable. Kids in the country start working earlier. Not like city kids."

"I didn't learn about the hard life of farmers until I lived on a military farm."

"Tea's ready." Gui's Wife handed a tall glass to Nina. "Life on a military farm is better than our farmers' life. We depended on the heavens. During years of poor weather we didn't have enough to eat. This is why we decided to sneak into Hong Kong. We sure have a better life here. When Gui comes home, you can ask him anything you want about Hong Kong."

***

The following day, Nina went into town by bus with the family. Gui first led her to the Office of Resident Affairs while his wife took their son to the mall. By the time they met again, Nina had received her resident card, and Gui had bought himself rubber boots, Gui's Wife her favourite floral cloth, and Bean, a toy gun. The following week, Nina helped Gui's Wife pick kelp on the beach. The collected kelp was then dried in the yard, and later, packed and stored. Every other week, Gui's Wife sold the kelp packages to a vendor. In the evening, Nina taught Bean how to read and write.

Several days later, Nina visited the American Consulate on Garden Street and requested an application for political asylum. On the same trip, she bought a Chinese-English dictionary from a bookstore. With the help of the dictionary, she worked on the application form for several days, filling it out with the required information:

Applicant: Nina Huang, born in 1949. Student, 1956-68. Thought reform on the Number Five Military Farm, 1968-1969. Arrived in Hong Kong on August 28, 1969.

Father: Jim Huang, born in 1924. Studied at West Point Academy, 1946-48. Returned to China and worked in the Nationalist Army, 1948-1949. Joined the PLA in 1949. Served in the Chinese Navy, 1955-1966. Persecuted because of his training in the U.S. and died in October 1966.

Mother: Min Liao, born in 1925. Medical doctor at Guangzhou Children's Hospital, 1950-1967. Labour Camp, 1967-69. Under house arrest, 1969-present.

She attached two additional pages describing why she was applying for political asylum and sent the package by registered mail. Several weeks later, she returned to the American Consulate for an interview.

She had written to Ray's grandmother in Guangzhou to ask about Ray, but she had not heard back. Her letter may have been intercepted or Ray's grandmother may not have dared to answer. The word "death" haunted her so much that she could not help but sob. Gui's Wife would pat her shoulder and say in a quivering voice, "Crying is no help." But she wept along with Nina, wiping her tears with the corner of her apron.

Often, Nina wondered about Hai. *How would he be punished if caught crossing the border? What is he doing if he is in Vietnam?* The questions were like worms eating away at her heart. She felt hollow, but she could not contact Hai or Dew for answers. Any letter from outside of China, to either of them, would create suspicion and make trouble for them. Praying for Hai and hoping he had survived was the only thing she could do.

Nina began to follow Voice of America's "English 900" program on the radio. Listening to the English conversations provided her with glimpses into American society and culture. She imagined her future in that society. She would not be forced to read Mao's or anybody else's works; she would not be afraid of expressing a different opinion; she would not be judged by her family background and be regarded as the offspring of the revolution's enemies. She would have the right to make choices in her own life. She wished someday, somewhere, that she might meet Hai again.

When, six months later, a package from the American Consulate arrived, Nina opened it with trembling hands. She had been granted a visa to enter the U.S. She was overcome with relief and sorrow. Tears streamed down her cheeks, and she could not keep her hand, which held the passport, from shaking.

"Don't go. Those blue-eyed and high-nosed people are scary," Gui's Wife said, her voice quivering. They had become close over the past six months. "You're educated and you will earn more money than us. You don't need to go," she pleaded, pulling on Nina's arm. "Stay here, with us."

Nina raised her head and looked deeply into Gui's Wife's eyes, knowing with certainty that she could not stay. The green sheet of paper that had unfolded in front of her, granting her asylum, looked shiny, as if a sparkling star had emerged in a starless sky.

FROG FISHING

ONE DAY AT NOON in early September of 1976, I stood on a ridge that bordered fields of rice paddies on the outskirts of a southern city in China and stared at the line hanging over the rice plants from the tip of my bamboo stick. I was fishing with Pearl for frogs during our two-hour lunch break. Once in a while I pulled my stick up and down, and the moth-like cotton shook around to lure a frog. The sun rose high in the sky and helped turn rice heads golden-yellow. The wind sometimes blew a gust of cool air – air that seemed to be whispering secrets.

"My God! A huge one!" Pearl's scream startled me. "Lotus, help me catch it!"

I raised my head and scanned the rice paddies, but I couldn't see Pearl. Had a giant frog dragged her into the water? I dropped my fishing rod and ran along the ridge in the direction of her voice. In front of me, locusts hopped on rice plants, and frogs jumped into the water.

Pearl was sprawled, face down on the ground, her arms outstretched, her hands pinning her grey jacket against the narrow muddy ridge.

"Be quick!" she shouted. "I can't hold on anymore."

When I bent over, my eyes met with hers – eyes that looked like those of a goldfish, pallid and desperate. Her face glistened with sweat.

I noticed a huge lump twitching under her jacket and imagined a big bowl of delicious soup. Excited, I inserted my hand under her jacket to pull the creature out. Finally, I touched something snappy and slick.

Fumbling around with my fingers, I managed to grab hold of two slippery legs.

"You can let go," I told Pearl.

As she loosened her hands, I pulled the wriggling thing out from under the jacket. It wasn't a frog but a pudgy, fleshy toad. Before I had time to examine my captive, a spurt of liquid shot from between its legs toward my face. Gasping in astonishment, I flung the still urinating toad into the air. The animal, like a tiny aircraft, arced up into the air, then shot down, and, with a loud slap, hit a large stone.

After I wiped my eyes with a handkerchief, I found the pitiful toad lying on its back, its grey belly up, probably dead.

"Do you hear the school bell?" asked Pearl, who rose from the ground.

I listened. It was our bell ringing. Glancing at my watch, I answered, "It's 1:19. We still have about forty minutes before the start of afternoon classses."

"Who's crazy enough to ring the bell that early today?" asked Pearl.

"Let's go back to see what's going on. I have a class to teach at two anyway," I answered.

We collected our two short bamboo sticks and a plastic bag full of small cotton puffs that we used for frog fishing, and hid them under a bush near a rice paddy for the next time. I smoothed my clothes and walked back to school with Pearl, empty-handed.

When we reached the playground, we saw that other teachers were walking into the auditorium. We caught up to them and followed them inside, where our principal already stood on the stage. His face was long and narrow and so sombre that we'd long ago nicknamed him Long Face.

Eight years earlier, as the leader of a poor farmers' group, Long Face had been sent to Grass Elementary School according to Mao's policy to remould the teachers. In Long Face's unique way of reading, he pronounced the word "monkey" as "money" and spelt "deadline" as "deadlion." In any case, he was an appointed principal, so who dared to correct him?

"Attention! You bourgeois teachers," the sad voice of Long Face echoed – he enjoyed using words from propaganda materials. "Our reddest, Red Sun … he's fallen from the sky, alas!" he sobbed.

"Chairman Mao?" I turned my head toward Pearl who sat next to me, and stared at her in disbelief.

She raised her eyebrows. "Dead?"

Then a dirge, punctuated with sobbing and whimpering, filled the auditorium. The grey-bellied toad came into my mind and a sense of mercy about death rose inside me. Before that moment, I'd often thought, like everyone in China, that Chairman Mao was immortal. "Long live Chairman Mao!" was the mantra heard everywhere in the country, all the time. Talking, even thinking, about the death of Mao was viewed as a sin, a crime.

The principal demanded we cancel all afternoon classes to begin the mourning process. Teachers were to organize the students into groups to make wreaths with white paper flowers for an altar and black armbands for everybody to wear.

After school, we created the altar on the stage in the auditorium where we'd hold a wake for Chairman Mao. The staff was divided into three-person groups. Each group would keep watch for a ten-hour shift until seven days had passed and Mao's soul had risen to the heavens.

I was partnered with Jade, a middle-aged teacher of Chinese language, and Baton, a young teacher of Physical Education. Often, Baton's ball missed the basketball ring, and the students would snicker at him behind his back.

That evening, according to the schedule, I walked into the auditorium for our assigned vigil at seven o'clock sharp. Jade was already seated in a chair facing the altar. Baton stood and leaned by a window, although all other seats were unoccupied. A lit cigarette between his fingers became shorter bit by bit as smoke drifted from his nose like fog in front of his face.

Jade waved at me to come over to her. I walked purposefully toward the altar and perched next to her. We sat tight without speaking for several hours. Jade was usually very talkative. Today she was silent. The door was ajar and the night breeze blew in, dissipating Baton's cigarette smoke. The white paper flowers and ribbons decorating the huge wreath trembled slightly with the breeze. A large, black Chinese character painted on the diamond-shaped piece of paper in the centre of the wreath read "the spirit of the dead." The surrounding ashen flowers poked out of the arrangement like grey bones. The word "dead" in the centre of the wreath seemed ready to leap out from the circle of grey bones.

The room was quiet and empty as if there were no human beings present. But my mind was fully occupied. One of the stories I'd heard from my nanny when I was a child stirred in my head: a black cat leapt over a coffin and made the corpse inside rise. *Would Mao climb out of his crystal casket?* I wondered.

It began raining outside. The earlier breeze was now a forceful wind. The indoor light looked like a blinking eye as the door to the auditorium swung open and then shut with each gust of wind that whipped around the building. I imagined a dead man climbing out of a coffin on the stage and jumping down to chase me. *Where could I go?* I asked myself. *Should I run around the chairs or escape from the auditorium?* I thought it might be better to stamp my feet on the floor and shout: *You are dead! You can't come out of the coffin.*

"Have you heard any news about Beijing?" Jade unexpectedly broke the silence.

Taken aback by her question, I shook my head. "No."

"Baton's gone out." She pointed to the door, her voice barely containing her excitement. "The Communist leaders in power have no future."

Is it safe? I glanced at the door and didn't see Baton. "The joy belongs to the people!" I hastily recited a verse from one of the Tiananmen Poems that I had heard through the grapevine. Even though the government had banned these poems, the people had spread them across China by word of mouth after the Tiananmen Incident in April. The government had suppressed the mass congregation in Tiananmen Square that had gathered to commemorate the late Premier Zhou and to criticize Mao's closest associates.

"I was in Beijing at that time, on Chang'an Avenue," Jade had much to say. "I found bloodstains in the cracks of the concrete tiles."

We exchanged whatever news we had; news that was quite different from what the newspapers reported. When Baton returned we sank back into speechlessness. Only the rain and wind filled the lifeless night.

***

A week later, the school returned to its routine. As usual, on Saturday afternoon all the teachers met in the main office for a weekly political meeting run by the school leaders.

After reading out loud an important article from the *People's Daily*, Long Face's gaze fell on the audience. "Teachers! Comrades! We ought to watch the new motion and direction of the class struggle in our school!" he repeated a passage from the article word for word. Finally he announced, "Some people have verbally attacked our Party's central leaders!"

Everyone in the room eyed one another in shock. We all knew that if a person was caught making unfavourable comments about any of the government's central leaders, he or she would have committed an anti-revolutionary crime and would most certainly be imprisoned.

"It was Jade and Lotus!"

My mind went blank. White spots appeared in front my eyes, and I felt dizzy, as if a stick had struck my head. I'd already heard about the arrests of people who talked against Mao's associates.

"Lotus!" Jade called out. "Did we attack the central leaders?"

My lips moved, but I was wordless until Pearl tugged the back of my blouse and urgently whispered, "Say '*no*'!"

Finally waking up from my confusion, I stood up and firmly said, "No, we did not!"

"Principal Wang, we need witnesses," Jade said. "Who heard us?"

"Alright." Long Face hesitated for a moment, as if he wanted to hide the identity of the informer, but in order to convince the audience, he was forced to confess. "Baton heard your vicious attacks."

"Did anyone else hear us talk that night?" Jade turned to Baton. She asked in a firm tone, "Baton, who else can prove what you've accused us of?"

"I can," Baton answered in a weak voice.

"One witness isn't enough." Jade looked directly at Long Face. "Chairman Mao said, 'If you haven't conducted an investigation, you have no right to make any assumption.' Principal Wang, why don't you ask other teachers?" She turned to the other listeners. "Has anybody ever heard Lotus and I discuss the central leaders?"

"Never!"

"Lotus seldom talks," said one.

"Maybe Baton got it wrong," said another.

At that moment, I noticed Long Face's puzzled eyes and Baton's speechless, half-opened mouth.

As the meeting finished, my jumping heart returned to its place. Jade and I had survived that round of political accusation.

***

Near the end of September, Pearl and I went frog fishing again. The rice paddies looked the same, although much had changed in the past weeks. Mao's death was like peeling paint on a house, eventually revealing its original colour.

"Pearl," I asked as I pulled a tiny puff of cotton from the bag and tied it to the end of the line of my fishing rod. "What program are you going to apply for if the entrance examinations for universities are re-established?" We'd been trained to teach in a two-year post-secondary program, but we never had a chance to go to university. I hoped that now we might get that chance.

"Mathematics!" she answered, without taking the time to think.

"Why? I thought you loved literature."

"People in arts have lots of trouble with politics." Pearl whipped her fishing rod over the rice plants. The cotton puff looked like a moth falling slowly and softly into the plants. "What about you?"

"I'd like to try archaeology. I like the idea of discovering ancient remains and bones." At that moment, I felt a twitch on my line. *A bite from a frog!* I yanked my rod sharply. Whoosh! A frog hung awkwardly on the line swinging in the air. My other hand stretched to grab it before it had a chance to wriggle off the line. I caught the little creature, its mouth exposed as it struggled.

The disgusting scene of Baton at the political meeting popped into my head. I pictured him gaping at Jade again. I wondered whether Baton would've reported on us if he'd known about the boomerang effect – he couldn't defend or support his accusation and so only humiliated himself. *Would the frog have opened its mouth to get the moth if it'd known it'd be caught?*

"Lotus! Why don't you put the frog in the bag? You almost killed it." Pearl's voice drew me back to the present.

The frog in my hand closed its wordless mouth. Its eyes puffed and stared blankly into the sky. *Poor thing!* I thought. I loosened my fingers and it dropped to the ground. The frog kicked around and then disappeared into the plants. The ribbit of other frogs rose here and there.

The sun remained in the high sky, and the rice heads had already become ripe. Once more, we threw in our lines, hoping to catch frogs in the rice paddies.

A WOMAN OF CHINA

A man by the age of thirty should have accomplished his goals.
– Ancient Chinese proverb

"MA … MAMA!" JUN CALLED out after waking.
"I'm here, baby!" Ting stopped unpacking to pick up the little girl from the crib.

In Ting's arms, Jun looked around, noticing nothing familiar except her mom's face. She mumbled, "Ho-mee. Ho-mee."

"Yes, this is our new home." Ting chuckled. With smiling eyes, she gazed at her two-year-old daughter, wondering if she really understood the meaning of "home." Their new home was impossibly cramped. It was a bachelor apartment allotted by her husband's university, and cluttered with a double bed, a crib, a stroller, two bookcases, and a desk. Several shelves, attached to any available space on the walls, were lined with books, magazines, jars, and other containers of different shapes.

After she set Jun beside the toy blocks on the bed, Ting continued opening the boxes and shelving their contents. She felt exhilarated about her new life. It was spring and she had just moved to Shanghai to rejoin her husband. She hummed as she pulled books out of the cardboard boxes. Her shoulder-length hair swung back and forth as she moved back-and-forth, shelving books. Later, she reminded herself, she would hang a clothesline across a wall corner. The line would be important on rainy days when she had to hang her daughter's cloth diapers to dry inside. She nicknamed the diapers of different colours and sizes, "Flags of a Thousand Countries."

Thump! Startled by the sound, Ting quickly raised her head and saw that Jun had tumbled from the bed as she tried to reach for a block that had fallen on the floor. "Oh my God!" Ting tried to control her voice and hurried to cradle Jun in her arms. The little girl opened her mouth to cry, but started giggling instead when Ting patted her back.

"Sweetie, are you hungry?" Ting's shoulders stopped shaking. Her hand touched Jun's stomach.

Jun nodded, her smile wide.

Ting placed Jun carefully on the floor with a few of the toy blocks. She passed her a cracker and began mixing rice powder, minced pork, and shredded vegetables with water. She cooked the mixture and then placed the pot in a sink of cold water to cool.

Not having a high chair, Ting settled Jun in the stroller and fed her. Jun grabbed the spoon from her mother and grinned, wanting to feed herself. Ting took another spoon and said in a sing-song voice, "You put one spoon into your mouth and I'll put in the other." Sometimes Jun pushed the spoon against her own cheeks or nose; at other times she would clang it on the stroller tray. Jun finished her meal – half of it decorating her face.

Half an hour later, the door opened, and Ting's husband, Dong, arrived from his day's work at the university.

"How was your day?" he asked, casting a glance at the crib after he laid his briefcase on the floor. "Is Jun still asleep?"

"She just dozed off after eating, or rather, wearing a meal."

"You're not done with these boxes, are you?"

"Almost, but not yet," answered Ting as she put another pan on the gas stove and began to stir-fry what was left of the pork with some fresh vegetables from the refrigerator. "Did you get any news from the daycare centre?"

"No. But I asked one of my colleagues for help since his mother works there." Dong patted his stomach. "We should get a spot any day now. How soon will supper be ready?"

"It's almost done."

Dong arranged a folding table in the small room for them to take their meal. They ate in silence, each lost in thought about what the future might bring.

***

Several days later, daycare for Jun secured, Ting walked into an office building that *Huangpu Daily* shared with a real estate company. Along the narrow hallway on the fifth floor she passed rooms filled with desks and office workers. Sunlight squeezed in through white blinds and danced on the walls. Finally, she spotted the personnel office. Smoothing her skirt, she turned the doorknob and entered the room with a timid smile on her face. It wasn't as hard as she thought to detail her qualifications to the welcoming face behind the counter.

The personnel officer handed her the note on which he had jotted down some of her information and directed her to the manager of the Editorial Department in the office across the hall. She was feeling more confident and knocked sharply on the door.

"Come in, please!" answered a genial man sitting behind a large desk, stacks of file folders in neat piles before him.

"I'm here for the job opening," Ting said as she entered the room and strode to the desk, handing over the note from the personnel officer.

The manager stood up and shook hands with Ting. "Sit down." He pointed to a chair, and picked up a tea mug from his desk. "You're young," he said, his eyes scrutinizing her. "So, you must have good eyesight."

Why does good eyesight matter? Ting asked herself. *For taking photos, perhaps?* She answered, "Yes, sure," and sat up straight.

The director smiled, placing his mug back on the desk after taking a sip of the tea.

"All right. I can offer you a job as a proofreader." Nodding, he looked beyond her to the door.

"But, Sir," Ting's throat was dry when she spoke, "I have several years experience reporting and editing at a weekly newspaper."

"Such a position is not available here." He eyed the door again. "I see from this note that you have just moved to Shanghai. It's impossible to find an equivalent position when you transfer to a big city. Think of proofreading as something good. You don't have to always be on the run and you can spend more time with your family, especially with your child – if you have one." His voice was firm.

Ting raised her eyebrows. Knowing she had no other choice, she said, "Okay, I accept the position."

The manager stood up, "Good. You can start right away. I'll take you to the office where you will be working."

As they entered a desk-filled room, Ting detected a change in the atmosphere. The workers' heads, like black mushrooms, rose and peeked out over stacks of paper. They responded to the manager's introduction, greeted Ting politely, and then each mushroom head dropped, one by one. Silence shrouded the office as a middle-aged woman gestured at Ting. "Come on in. This is your desk," she said briskly, placing some work in front of her. After the manager left, the mushroom heads reappeared. Pleasant chatter flowed across the paper stacks. Ting sat down and began her first day proofreading freshly printed sheets.

At the end of the day, she boarded a crowded trolley bus that had standing room only. She positioned herself in front of a window so she could see Nanjing Road West, the most prosperous commercial area in Shanghai. Neon lights on the glass doors and windows of stores cast shimmering rays of light on the bustle of shoppers coming and going. Ting blinked her eyes in order to tell real people from mannequins.

***

Ting hated to have her ambition buried in proofreading, but she enjoyed reading. Whenever she had spare time, she read novels and poetry and sometimes even academic and scientific journals. At lunch, she read a report on housing in Shanghai, written for the 1987 International Year of Housing. Eyes wide, she stared at the photo accompanying the piece. "Have you seen this story about the shabby and crowded living conditions in a suburb of Shanghai?" she asked her colleagues. "I can't believe this old man has lived in a two-square metre room for thirty years."

"Mine isn't much better. We are a family of four and we live in a small apartment that is about thirty-two square metres," the person at the next desk responded.

"This is reality in Shanghai," another sighed.

Ting fell silent, thinking: *My living space is much bigger than that poor old man's. It's five square metres per person!*

Every evening, after she finished cleaning up and taking care of the laundry and tucking her daughter into bed, she immersed herself in books. Sometimes, she even read books in English using a dictionary. Once in a while, Dong would tease her. "You live more like a student than I do." Dong was studying part-time for his doctoral degree while teaching a course in Chinese history.

Ting considered taking graduate courses as well. She thought that with a Master's she might have a better chance of getting a job as a journalist again. She picked up some information about advanced studies in journalism at the university and discussed the possibility with Dong. "I think I can pass the entrance exams for the graduate program."

"What do you mean?" Dong asked, looking at her as though he hadn't understood what she just said. "Who will take care of Jun if you go to school?"

"She can still go to daycare during the day and we can take turns looking after her in the evenings, so that we both have time to study."

"No. It's not good for the kid. She needs a mother." Dong was insistent.

"But I need a career," Ting said quietly, her eyes fixed on his.

"I know what's in your head. But it's impossible for both of us to develop careers. Otherwise, neither of us will come along."

"Why can't I try?"

"You know why. You're a woman."

"And what's the matter with that?" Ting said, barely able to hide the annoyance in her voice. "Are you suggesting women are inferior?"

"Something like that."

"I'm as smart as you are."

"Men are more easily accepted in society," said Dong, a wry smile on his face. "Listen, it's a man's world not a woman's world. 'Mankind,' remember, not 'womankind'!" Dong smirked. "Only when a man has distinguished himself can his wife be honoured."

"I don't believe in Confucian tradition."

"Believe it or not, it's a fact."

Ting's eyes dimmed. She realized what Dong said was partly true. She did not know of any successful marriages that involved careers for both the husband and wife. A hard-working couple had to sacrifice family life for a man's career. She remembered the ancient Chinese proverb: *A man by the age of thirty should have accomplished his goals.* And a woman of China was expected to support her husband's ambitions and help him achieve those goals.

As a mother, Ting also had a duty to think about her daughter. Pity for her daughter began in the labour room once the nurse announced, "It's a baby girl!" The love that grew afterwards was always huddled in the shadow of that pity. Ting hated to think that Jun might experience the same obstacles as she had. She understood that women had to climb over more barriers in order to stand alongside men at the same level. With a clear picture in mind of the obstacles Jun would face, she resolved to raise her daughter with care and ensure that she would be well-educated. As a wife, she also truly hoped her husband would succeed in his career. For these reasons, she convinced herself she had to give up her desire to further her own education.

The couple busied themselves in their daily routines. Their family life remained a stale pool in a deep valley in early summer. Only Jun's babbling made joyful ripples.

***

One hot and damp Friday in July, Ting proofread an extra article; it was an emergency, the manager said. Exhausted, she dragged herself to the bus stop and back to the apartment. As she walked down the hallway, she could hear Jun crying and smell burned rice. She quickly pulled the door open and saw her daughter pushing a bottle of milk away while Dong stood, red-faced, his hand holding a steaming pot.

"Remember your daughter?" Dong shouted at the sight of Ting, flinging the pot of rice to the floor.

"Control your stinking, boorish manner!" Ting shouted back, inflamed with rage.

"Why are you late? Where have you been? I had to pick up Jun after the daycare called and said you couldn't."

"Where do you think I was? I was working! Why should I have to do everything? Why can't you pick up Jun sometimes?"

"*This* is *your* job!" Dong said, his face burning with anger, his body lunging toward her. "And it should be your priority!"

"You stupid man!" Tears streaming down her face, Ting took Jun in her arms and stormed out of the apartment. She could still hear him shouting as she ran to the bus stop.

Ting and Jun got on the first bus that came by. It was crowded but a young man offered Ting his seat. After thanking him, she sat down holding Jun in her lap. The people around her looked sleepy, but Jun was wide-eyed with curiosity, standing up on her mother's lap and pressing her face on the window, her hands waving at the people outside. Ting held her daughter's legs securely and leaned her rigid back against the seat. Her eyes stared at the seat in front of her. The sweat on her forehead glistened under the soft, yellowish light of the bus and slowly trickled down her pale face.

Half an hour later, she reached her destination. After being buzzed in, she climbed the stairs to the sixth floor with Jun in her arms, stopping every three or four steps to hold her daughter on her knee for a brief rest. Finally, she reached the apartment she was looking for and knocked on the door. An elderly woman appeared and looked at Ting expectantly. "What's wrong?"

"Aunt Yue, Dong and I…," Ting said, choking back tears. "He yelled at me."

Aunt Yue gently took Jun from Ting's arms and carried the little girl to a couch. "Come in, come in, and sit down. Now, what happened?"

"I always pick up Jun from the daycare and fix supper," said Ting, sitting down next to Jun. "Except for today. Today I had to stay at work later than usual to finish proofing one more article. Dong was so mad that he had to pick Jun up that he lost his temper."

"So you haven't had your supper yet."

"Right. And Jun needs milk, too."

"I have some powdered milk. Just give me a minute to prepare it." Aunt Yue walked to the kitchen and returned with a glass of milk in her hand, placing it on the coffee table near the couch. She said, "I have some leftovers in the fridge. You can have them if you want."

"I'm not hungry, but I do have to make some noodles for Jun." Ting took the glass of milk and helped Jun drink it. A few moments later the noodles were ready and Ting fed them to her daughter. It wasn't long before Jun was sound asleep.

Ting looked around her aunt's cozy living room and relaxed in an arm-chair near the only window. "Aunt, don't you think Dong is selfish?"

"Why?" The aunt placed two chairs next to the edge of the couch, so Jun wouldn't roll onto the floor, and then sat on the wingback chair next to Ting.

"Dong was angry with me because he had to take Jun home and make supper. When the manager asked me to stay, I phoned the daycare and asked them to let Dong know he had to pick up Jun. Why was he so angry? I do all the housework and take care of Jun practically by myself. I have a job, too."

"As a wife and a mother, you can't escape your family duties."

"But he should share half of those duties." Ting glared at her aunt, expecting a more supportive answer.

"Ideally, yes. But in most of the families I know, the women do the majority of the housework. Maybe it's a kind of tradition that women have to follow unless…"

"Unless what?"

"Unless women remain single, like me." Aunt Yue chuckled. "I don't need to do anything for a husband or a child."

"That's why you are successful in your career," Ting said apprecia-tively.

"But I lost the opportunity to enjoy having my own family as a re-sult."

"Do you have any regrets?"

"In my time, it was the only choice I had because I wanted to study medicine more than having a family."

"Things haven't changed in my time," sighed Ting.

"Think about your life positively. Dong is well-educated and ambi-tious. I think he really cares for you and Jun."

"Do you think so?" Ting looked at her aunt quizzically. "If he loved us, he wouldn't have reacted the way he did. And he would let me go to graduate school, which would help me get a better job. Why can't I have a career too?"

"I don't want to judge, Ting. It's your choice," Aunt Yue said as she patted Ting on the shoulder. "When you are a wife and mother, you have to give up a part of you. This is what I have learned from life and also why I never wanted to get married."

When the telephone rang, Aunt Yue answered. "Yes, she's here." She signalled to Ting. "It's for you."

Ting took the phone and heard Dong's voice, "I apologize, Ting. Are you still mad at me? Please come home."

"Are you really sorry?" Ting listened for a while to Dong's excuses and then said, "Okay, I'll come home tomorrow. Then we can talk it over."

After hanging up, Ting turned to her aunt and said, "I'm starving. Can I have a bite of something?"

Ting's aunt chuckled and opened the refrigerator.

***

The summer passed by.

One evening in September, Ting turned on the radio after Jun had fallen asleep. Eager to learn more about the United Nations' Fourth World Women's Conference that was convening in Beijing, she searched the dial for Voice of America as it provided news not given by the Xinhua News Agency. To her surprise, she heard one of the conference participants call for Chinese lesbians to join the women's struggle for equal rights with men. *Chinese lesbians?* Ting had never heard anyone talk about this. *Women who love other women? And have nothing to do with men?*

Dong didn't get home until after 10:00 p.m. He had been busy attending to students who needed extra help. Ting handed him a glass of iced tea. "Do you think there are lesbians in China?"

"What a strange question!" Dong replied, yawning. "I don't know anything about that," he added, heading toward the bathroom.

Ting tried to continue the conversation after Dong came back. "I just heard about them on Voice of America. There is a big women's conference in Beijing. Women from the West are asking Chinese lesbians to join them."

"How can women have sex with women? It's strange and ridiculous. Let's go to bed." Dong took off his T-shirt.

"I'm wondering what their rights are," Ting said. "They want equal rights."

"Rights?" Dong laughed. "What rights?" He climbed into bed. "Come on. It has nothing to do with us. Don't be bothered."

"I'm curious," said Ting as she lay beside Dong. "Lesbians don't marry men, you know. Maybe they can do whatever they want. I'd like to know more about them."

His warm hands were already cupping her breasts. "Curiosity killed the cat," he murmured, nuzzling her neck.

Ting suddenly felt like a cat caught by Dong. Her body became stiff. The words *women, lesbian, curiosity,* and *cat,* began spinning in her head.

Dong's body was on top of her, heavy and sticky. She felt uncomfortable but did not push him away.

"Are you dead or what?" Dong's voice pulled her back to the present. "Don't you like this?"

Ting turned her head aside on the pillow. "Not really. I'm feeling a little pain."

"Pain? Since when?"

"What? Are you suggesting I'm making this up because I have no interest in sex with you? Why don't you just call me a lesbian then?" Ting pushed Dong off and turned her body away from him.

"How would I know?" grumbled Dong. Exhausted, he dropped off into dreamland.

The Clock Tower of the Customs House echoed in the distance. It was already midnight, and Ting was still awake. Her thoughts flashed to what she had heard about Canada, a country whose doors were open to immigrants. Many people in Shanghai applied for immigration via the Canadian Consulate. *Are women equal to men there? Lesbians too? Are they successful in their careers, and married too? Are they lesbians because they don't want to cater to men?* These questions preoccupied her.

Perhaps I should immigrate, Ting thought. *I'd have a chance to find out what kinds of rights and freedoms the women enjoy over there, and, I can become one of those women.* Excited about this thought, she got up and searched in one of her drawers for a flyer she had received just that day from one of her co-workers who had family in Canada. The flyer was about immigrating to Canada.

She took a good look at the flyer. Then she took a good look at the date on her digital watch: it was September 26, 1995. Like thunder cracking in the sky, she suddenly remembered: *Oh my! I'm thirty years old today.* Thoughtfully, she asked herself, *And what have I accomplished?* She gripped the flyer in one hand. But the only thing that came to mind was that she had forgotten to ask Dong to buy her a birthday cake.

TEN YUAN

I WORKED AS AN APPRENTICE at an armament factory in the early 1970s, during the middle of the Cultural Revolution. People didn't talk about money because the revolution was more important. But I still kept my fingers crossed, hoping to be promoted to a second level within two years, so my pay would increase by ten yuan a month. Ten dimly shining coins would make a nice sound, and buy me a pair of pointy-toed shoes.

In a workshop, I laboured with vises, wrenches, hacksaws, nails, and bolts to repair or change machine parts. Sometimes I needed to cut an iron bar or bend a steel rod, my hands always greased with oil. It would've rained dark oil if I had slapped my hands in the air. Sometimes I had to clean broken machine parts in a metal tub of oil, examining them, like a nurse who had to rinse a wound.

Our factory produced cannon shells—shells that would subsequently be filled with explosives in yet another factory. The product was considered confidential, and that was why the factory had been built in this isolated rocky valley. We worked and lived in concrete buildings, and rarely caught sight of trees or birds. I liked to think that the birds were smart and knew that bullets could kill them and that cannonballs were much more powerful than bullets.

Our factory, for various reasons, often had to stop production. The whole country was involved in the Revolution, and sometimes denounced engineers or technicians were not allowed to work. When this happened we simply stopped working; there was no one to solve problems on the assembly line. Sometimes we didn't have electricity, and other times, the materials we needed had been delayed in transport.

When we had nothing to do, we played cards in the workshop. Why not? Everybody got paid no matter if he worked or not. Some of us even napped on benches. One skinny guy always perched himself near a window, hoping to catch a glimpse of the few women who worked in the factory walking by. Within ten square kilometres, there were no villages or towns, so it was difficult for us bachelors to find girlfriends. This skinny guy would sit there all day, when he had the chance. We named him Flower Geek, and his window the Ogling Stage.

One day, when the electricity went out, and all the machines stopped turning, the foreman patted my shoulder and said, "Tell us a story, Lee!" He called me by the name the Communist Party secretary had used a year earlier, on that first day, when he had given a speech to all the new workers. After the tedious speech, he took a roll call from a piece of paper in his hand.

"Lee Ma!"

I remembered looking around to see who shared my family name. Nobody answered.

"Lee Ma! I'm calling you!" The Party secretary had then pointed at me. "Why don't you answer?"

His words had thrown me for a loop. "I … my … name is Tea Ma."

"It's Lee Ma on my list!" he had barked.

What could I do if that's how he had chosen to read my name? Since then, some of the men had teased me, using my new name. "Lee Ma!" One would point at me as if he were the Party secretary, his arm cutting the air. "If you don't answer, I'll behead you!" It always made everyone laugh.

Now our foreman called me again, "Lee!" Holding a cup in the crook of his little finger like a rich woman, he said, "Tell us the story, 'The Sign of the Four'!" The foreman knew I had read a lot of Sherlock Holmes, so he always asked me to retell Holmes' adventures with the other men. This brought some pleasure to our boring and somewhat dispirited life. At that time, Sherlock Holmes's books were banned like most other books, but I had a way of sneaking them into the factory. Storytelling wouldn't get me into hot water if nobody blew the whistle.

"On his deathbed, an old, very wealthy gentleman held the hands of his son and daughter," I began. "He told them about his adventures and the fortune he had made in his travels to India and then brought back to England. He was about to whisper to his children where his treasure was hidden, when…" I paused, trying to heighten the suspense.

Striking my arm, one fellow asked, "When *what?*"

"His eyes wildly scanned the room, and the terror in his voice rose as he yelled, 'Keep him out!'" For extra effect, I opened my mouth wide, squeezed my eyes shut, and made a strange, gurgling sound.

"Keep *who* out? A ghost?" asked one listener. Someone jumped from his bench to come and sit beside me.

"Go on," he urged.

I told them that a horned and bearded man was pressing his nose against the window of the old man's room. My listeners murmured among themselves. I paused to take a sip of tea from a mug that one of them had just passed to me, and then continued the story…

On yet another day, when all the machines stopped turning, we decided to play poker. Easing ourselves to the ground in a circle, we shuffled a set of cards and six of us started to play.

"Gee!" Flower Geek suddenly called out. "Look!"

I looked up from the cards in my hand. Flower Geek had risen from the Ogling Stage and was boogying toward us.

"Tea!" a female voice burst out behind me. "Do you have a minute?" Startled, I turned around and to my surprise, Cao, a girl apprentice from another workshop, had entered the room, carrying a tray full of steaming mugs of tea.

Cao always took care of her appearance. At that time, girls had few choices for clothes. On this day, she wore a blazer and a loose, dark blue skirt. In our eyes, she looked like a beauty out of a fairy tale.

She seldom bothered to speak to us young fellows, so I wondered about the real reason for her sudden appearance in our room. *She must have something important to say,* I thought.

"What's the matter?" I asked calmly, not wanting to seem too interested or too curious.

"Can you find *Dream of the Red Chamber?*" She looked at me and waited for me to say yes.

"Why? *Dream of the Red Chamber* has been banned." Curiosity occupied the whole of me. "Can't you recite Chairman Mao's quotations? Why do you need that book?"

"Why not? Chairman Mao said '*Dream of the Red Chamber* is the encyclopaedia of Chinese feudalism.' Judging by your answer, it seems you don't know this particular quotation," replied the girl, her smile gently mocking me. "My supervisor, Sister Guo, asked me to find a copy of *Dream of the Red Chamber*."

"Sister Guo? Alright. I'll let you know next week," I replied. *If Sister Guo, as a Party member, dares to read that book, why shouldn't I?*

"Please," Cao said, "thank you! I'll expect to hear from you then." She glided away. All of our eyes focused on her behind. A week later I found the book for Cao. After that she came to my workshop several times to either borrow or return books. That was how we became friends.

***

Time flew. I had been working as an apprentice for two years. As the time for promotion was around the corner, the factory organized an activity of long-distance jogging as a military manoeuvre for us young workers. In those years, success in the activities organized by the Communist Party was far more important than attaining other work skills. I knew that our performance in this manoeuvre was a crucial measurement of whether we would get a raise of ten yuan in the near future. Excited, we prepared our knapsacks and readied ourselves for the test.

Because he had applied to join the Communist Party, Flower Geek got appointed as our leader. The Party gave him this assignment as a trial of his faith and loyalty. He certainly didn't want to miss out on the opportunity, so he became unusually sociable, speaking to this person and patting that one on the shoulder.

The jogging drill would last five days, and we would pass through three towns. Altogether, sixty-seven workers, composed of fifty-nine young men and eight young women, joined the journey. Flower Geek played favourites with the girls and granted privileges to them. He would, for example, give them more free time and never blamed them when they were late or when they chatted during political meetings.

Although all the young men were unhappy about that, we didn't dare have words with him. And besides, we were happy to have more women in the factory.

On the third evening, we reached a five-road intersection at the centre of Circle Town. Then we were given some time off for supper. After the arduous workout, we were like famished wanderers. In threes and fives, we rushed into the several small restaurants the town offered. Cao and two other girls followed our group into a diner for supper. Flower Geek joined us, too.

I was so hungry that I stumbled to the counter. The aroma of the food made my mouth water more. I bought eight steamed stuffed buns and two bowls of soup. Relaxing in a chair, I gulped down all the buns, although they didn't taste that great. My hunger disappeared, and I forgot the fatigue I had gone through, as well as the purpose. Stuffed like a packed sack, I found it difficult to move my body.

I noticed that Cao was looking at me disapprovingly, and whispering something to the girls who were with her. I felt ashamed that I had wolfed down my food so quickly. I tried to make a joke of it. I told my companions the story of Dame Sun in the ancient Chinese novel, *Water Margin*. In this novel, Dame Sun and her husband ran an underground hostel in the woods. The couple killed several guests in their lodge where Dame Sun sold steamed buns stuffed with the flesh of the dead. "Maybe that's what we've just eaten," I said, smiling broadly, finally managing to get a few laughs.

When we finally returned to the town's school where we would sleep overnight, Flower Geek ordered us to attend a political studies session in the hall. He looked around the audience and then started his speech, "Comrades! Chairman Mao teaches us to 'fight against selfishness and criticize revisionism.' Now, let's do self-criticism one by one."

When my turn came, I criticized my selfishness: "Today, I used up my money and food coupons forgetting that two-thirds of the people in the world are short of food." Upon hearing a few snickers from the audience, I added, "I've made up my mind to correct my blunder, because I want to become a real working-class member who liberates the suffering people of the world."

Flower Geek watched me with his observant eyes, as if I were one of the women he had ogled. His gaze made my arms break out in goosebumps.

We returned to the workshop the following weekend.

On Monday morning, as I arrived at the workshop, a person from the security sector entered the room and asked me to report to the office.

I wondered what the reason might be. A dark cloud descended on me as I dragged my feet to the office.

"Tea Ma," the sector leader cleared his throat as soon as I entered the office and stood in front of him. "What did you do during the workout drill? Time for you to confess honestly without any tricks!"

"What?" I blundered. I wasn't entirely sure what he was referring to. Remembering the eight buns I had eaten during the trip, I made my confession: "I consumed too much food; a sort of waste of food."

"Don't try my patience!" After mashing a cigarette butt in an ashtray, the leader questioned again, "What did you say when you ate the buns in the restaurant?" He banged the desk and roared, "Get pardoned if you confess and get punished if you don't!"

The sudden shout gave me a startle. The scene in the restaurant flashed back into my mind. Yes, I had made a remark about the buns. I finally understood what this was about.

I said, "I made a joke."

"A joke? What did you joke about?"

"I said the buns tasted sour, a bit like human flesh."

"You've blackened our socialistic society." His eyebrows raised, and he continued to bawl, "You bastard! Don't you know that cannibalism was only practiced in the old society?"

"I goofed up," I said, lowering my voice and head at the same time. "I didn't mean anything by it."

He pointed at me and yelled, "Don't make my blood boil! We'd have put you behind bars if you were not from a worker's family!"

My hair stood on end when I heard these words, and I couldn't think straight. I blamed Circle Town and the diner, and the ugly waitress, and the sour buns.

"We've decided to suspend you from work for three days," he said. I was stunned and did not respond. The leader added, "Go back to your dorm and write a self-criticism report. Thursday morning you must read your report in front of everybody."

My head was throbbing when I staggered to the dorm. I entered the room I shared with three others and plopped into a chair. I realized that I was trembling. Staring at the only table, I saw nothing interesting but a couple of chipped mugs. Thankfully, my roommates weren't around to see me. It was the first time I was ever in the room alone. I lay down on my bed wondering why Chairman Mao hadn't banned Lu Xun's works. I remembered that in Lu Xun's novel, *A Madman's Diary*, the protagonist was a madman who discovered that his elder brother liked the taste of human flesh. The madman came to believe that he, too, would be eaten by his brother and other cannibals. Eventually I fell asleep and had a strange dream. I saw Lu Xun behind bars, his eyes opened wide. Dame Sun was carrying a plate of steamed buns stuffed with human flesh. Laughing eerily, she picked one up and offered it to Lu Xun. "Why don't you try one?" At that moment, I saw the skinny face of Flower Geek pressing against my dusty window, his nose white and squashed flat on the glass.

"Help!" I opened my mouth but couldn't make any sound. Suddenly I heard a young woman's voice. "Tea, wake up! I've brought you some tea."

I opened my eyes. My foreman was standing next to my bed, his face sweaty. Beside him was Cao, a sweet smile on her face. "What are you doing here?" I asked.

"I want to make sure you don't hang yourself," the foreman said with a chuckle. "Listen, nobody in the workshop wants to speak to Flower Geek. Cao heard what happened and asked me to bring her here."

I sat up and looked at my watch. It was almost 2:00 p.m., and my stomach was growling.

"I brought you some biscuits." Cao placed a paper box on the table next to a cup of hot tea. "Chairman Mao teaches us, 'We must see our achievements and brightness in times of difficulty.' You should look at the good side of the matter. Don't get too depressed."

"But I am depressed," I said to Cao. "I'm having a hard time seeing the good side of all this."

"Remember the Chinese fable of the old man who lost his horse? He lost one horse, but gained two things later."

Sure. I remembered the fable. The old man's missing horse came back with another horse. Then his son fell off the new horse, and because he broke his leg in the fall, he didn't have to go to war and risk dying in battle like most of the other young men from the village.

"Okay, okay…Thanks a bunch. Take a seat," I said, grabbing a chair for Cao from a corner of the room while I tried to fathom how Mao's "good side" theory could apply to my situation.

"No, thanks. I've got to go back to work," said Cao. "But I'll see you later, okay?" Her smile was warm and beautiful.

My spirits lifted. I smiled back at her, my eyes following her out of the room, and when she turned to look back at me, her hand on the door frame, her eyes sparkling, my heart skipped a beat. *A loser doesn't always lose. I can be marked or eaten by Flower Geek. But I've gained the heart of Cao.*

Suddenly Flower Geek rushed past her, stumbling into the room. "How are you, Cao?" Without waiting for her to respond, he turned to me and said, "It's not my fault, you know. It was a matter of business, and I had to tell them the truth."

"Oh, go to hell!" the foreman growled and left, taking Cao with him.

I turned away from Flower Geek, opened up the paper box of biscuits, and munched away. "Leave me alone," I said to him, brushing the crumbs from my lips.

Later, I read the self-criticism report I had been asked to write at an assembly of all the workers in the factory. I didn't feel too bad. Many of them looked at me with sympathy in their eyes.

My expectation of becoming a second-level worker became a pipe dream. I got ten yuan *less* per month than my peers for a whole year. That was worth twenty-four pointy-toed shoes! Flower Geek became a genuine Party whip, and was promoted to work in the security office.

For a long time, my stomach churned with butterflies each time I saw steamed buns. But, to this day, I never tire of Cao's fried rice.

BALLOONS

THE COOL JULY BREEZE blew lightly along the rocky seaside in St. John's, Newfoundland. The sunshine slipped through the green branches of the poplar trees and flickered on a red-roofed house. A white arched gate rose over a path that connected the front court to a dark green lawn. Bright balloons had been strung from tree to tree across the lawn toward the house, like cheerful smiling faces bobbing up and down over the guests at Patricia's wedding reception.

Among the crowd, Suyun sipped the scarlet wine as she gazed at the balloons. Red, blue, green, white, yellow, orange, and pink – colours formed many rainbows as they danced with the sun. Their twinkling colours reminded her of her childhood, and eventually wound their way into a black hole in her memory – the summer of 1969.

***

In an endless field near the border between China and Russia, several combines, partly filled with unthreshed wheat, lay still under the skin-scorching sun.

"Give up your balloon! I'm ordering you!" shouted a boy of about eight. With one hand scratching his dirty hair and the other brandishing a red willow branch, he pointed at a five-year-old girl sitting on the ground.

"Wh …why?" asked the girl, trying to hold back her tears with a firm voice. "This is my balloon. My brother made it for me. I won't give it to you!"

"My father is a leader. He gives orders to your father so I get to give you orders. Obey!" shouted the boy. He whipped the branch in the air. *Whoosh!* The dust swirled.

"Give the balloon to Longbin! Give it!" screamed several other children who had come closer.

The little girl gripped her red balloon, which was just a beach ball, dyed with red ink, and bound with a plastic strip to a metal wire.

"No. I won't!"

The boy pulled the ball with a ferocious yank that tore the wire away. He pulled so hard that he lost his balance and almost fell back on his behind. The children burst out laughing and the boy's cheeks flushed with anger. In a rage, he hit the girl's hands with his fist and shouted, "I'll beat you up! You are nothing but the brat of a landowner!"

The girl slackened her hands and let go of her red balloon. She prostrated her body on the ground. With her hands covering her eyes, she cried.

"A Kazakh's coming!" screamed the children as they scattered. "Kazakhs" were the native people their parents referred to as kidnappers or killers.

A hand patted her shoulder. "Why are you crying?"

Looking up through the cracks between her fingers, the girl saw the suntanned face of a Kazakh lad.

He spoke gently. "Don't be afraid. I won't hurt you. Here, take this," he said, passing her a tomato from a large basket he carried on his arm.

The girl hesitated at first, and then accepted the tomato, biting into it eagerly. She swallowed the cool, sweet juice, and her hot throat felt better.

"I'm Suyun. Longbin's robbed me of my balloon!"

Suyun pointed to her slashed and deflated red ball lying on the ground. The ball's red ink reflected a strange golden hue from the sun.

"You can't do anything about it and should go home now," said the boy. "Your parents may be looking for you."

Suyun nodded and hurriedly stood up. The sun had dropped behind the mountain range that rose from the edge of the quiet fields. "Thank you for your tomato," she said, smiling weakly.

After she flapped the dirt off her top and pants, she rushed toward home. As she approached the farm compound, she heard Chairman Mao's words set to music booming from a high-volume loudspeaker, "A revolution is an insurrection, an act of violence by which one class overthrows another."*

***

"Suyun, do you like balloons?" A pleasant female voice drew her back to the present. Suyun turned toward Patricia's smiling face. She was wearing an elegant, pink silk dress. Her light red hair shone in the sunshine, and her hand held a wineglass.

"Oh yes. I've loved balloons since I was a child."

"Me, too. I even tried to fly with a huge balloon when I was a first grader…" At that moment, Patricia spied more guests streaming through the gate. "Sorry, I've got to greet them. Enjoy yourself."

"All right," Suyun grinned. "I'll see you later."

As she watched Patricia walk away, she recalled the first time she attended Patricia's class. The course was on journalism and truth, and Patricia had flipped opened a copy of the university journal and raised it to the class. "Look," she had said, pointing to the article she wanted the class to read. "This article, entitled 'Special Treat,' is woven with gender discrimination."

Suyun carefully read the article but could not identify its gender discrimination. After class, she went to Patricia's office to ask her for some help.

Patricia had underlined one sentence in the article: "According to feminism, the existing social roles between genders start with socialization during children's growth." Then she explained to Suyun, "This sentence implies that functions in women's brains are different from those in men's brains so that women's abilities are different from men's."

Suyun remembered Patricia asking her earlier in class, "In ancient China, there is a saying, 'Look after your husband when he is studying,' right?"

Suyun had recognized the expression. It meant that the wife respected her husband and tried to help him when he studied.

"Yes," she had nodded.

"If you think that taking care of your husband is your 'duty,'" Patricia had said, looking at Suyun carefully. "Would you pursue a graduate degree for yourself?"

"As a child I was always told that 'women hold up half of the sky.'" Looking at Pat's surprised face, Suyun then added, "I also learned 'the enemy without guns still exists.'"

"The enemy without guns still exists? What is that?" Patricia had been puzzled.

"It refers to the enemy of the revolution," Suyun had explained. "My father is from a type of 'enemy' family. My elder brother was not allowed to attend high school as a result. That made me extremely eager to go to college."

Patricia had seemed to weigh these words carefully. Then she took several books from her bookshelf. "If you are interested in exploring some feminist theory, you can read these."

***

After the wedding reception, Suyun returned to her room in residence. In her mailbox, she was pleased to find a letter from her father. Once inside her apartment, she smoothed out the paper and began reading.

May 11, 1996
Suyun,

I used to think I'd better not breathe a word about my past. As you've asked me again and again about my family, I'm going to show my scars this time. My father was Shenyu Ren. Before 1949, he was a landowner and an administrator for the local nationalist government. After the Communist Party took power, he was jailed because he didn't want to surrender.

He had been labelled an obstinate landowner and was executed. My mother hanged herself after suffering from many humiliating denunciation meetings. My elder brother, Xianlin, a journalist for the nationalists' Central Daily, disappeared in 1950, before my father was put behind bars, and his house and properties were taken from him. Some people said he was in hiding somewhere. If so, why after all this time, has he never reappeared? Maybe he died during the chaotic period when the nationalists withdrew from Chongqing before the Communists' takeover.

Disaster fell on my family when I turned fifteen. I was a boarding-school student in Chongqing. One day, a friend risked his life to tell me that the militia in my hometown had decided to lock me up and put me into a denunciation meeting. Afraid of being unable to survive the struggle, I left the school right away. With a small bag, I fled to the remote northwest area of China. That was how I ended up in Xinjiang Province.

Several decades later, my family was pardoned, and I was declared a wronged victim. But it hasn't made a great difference. My parents are gone; my brother has vanished. I myself suffered from discrimination for so many years. I only wish for you and your brother to have decent and peaceful lives.

Your mother and I are fine. Your brother, along with his wife and daughter, spend every weekend with us.

My best wishes for your studies.

Your father, Xianpu

After reading her father's letter, Suyun felt tears fill her eyes. An afternoon in September 1976 appeared in her mind.

***

On a dusty school playground, the elementary students used hoes to mix soil with finely cut dry hay and water. They hummed some lyrics from the 1940s – lyrics that described the miserable life of brick makers: "We are making bricks today and we will make bricks tomorrow. From morning 'til evening we produce mud blocks." The melody sounded cheerful when the students sang it with laughter. This was a labour class for sixth graders. Everybody practiced making bricks by moulding the well-mixed mud. Among them was Suyun who bent over and carefully removed a mould from a brick. The day was hot and her face was red from the sun; some strands of her hair were wet and clinging to her forehead. She pointed her finger at the bricks as she counted them. *I've got my twentieth done.* She exhaled, and joined in the singing: "Our backs hurt, and waists ache. Making bricks to earn our –." Suddenly, several large clumps of mud slammed into her bricks, turning them into a shapeless mass. When she turned her head around to see who had thrown the mud, another wet lump splattered on her shoulder and muddy water streamed down her face.

"Stop!" she shouted.

"Landowner's doggy, shut up!" roared back a boy.

One girl attempted to judge the situation. "Weidong, you're to blame because you started it first."

"You evil girl! You stinking capitalist! Go back to Shanghai!" taunted the boy with his arms up in the air.

"A triumph! Dahan! Fight against landowners and anti-revolutionaries until the end!" Another boy supported his friend by shaping a mud ball and throwing it toward the girl who had defended Suyun.

"Chairman Mao teaches us, 'If you do not beat down all reactionaries, they will not fall.' Beat them down!" Several boys and girls recited Mao's words, urging the boys on.

Another five or six clumps of mud flew toward Suyun and the other girl. Some missed their targets and hit the wrong person. Then those who had been hit joined in the turmoil of clay: wet earth flew in all directions. Cheers, curses, and sobs drifted through the limbs of the birch trees that circled the playground.

The school principal, a middle-aged man with a straw hat, unexpectedly appeared in the middle of the warfare. "Girls and boys! Stop fighting!" A few lumps of the clay still flew, seeking their targets. The principal shouted, "Chairman Mao … he has passed away!"

The fighters froze and the mudslinging stopped suddenly. Children turned to the principal, their mud-streaked faces confused and frightened. Terrified, Suyun thought. *Wasn't he supposed to live forever? What do we do now without Chairman Mao?*

***

Staring at her father's letter, Suyun wondered whether it might be possible to find her missing uncle via the Internet.

Exhilarated by the idea, she wrote a message using the five "Ws" formula—"who, what, where, when, and why." Then she pulled up some online newsgroups – Chinese Newsgroup, Chinese Culture group,

Taiwan News, and Politics of Hong Kong – and she posted her message to these groups with hope.

Days went by and no message appeared. Her hope shrank. Perhaps it had been foolish to think she could actually find him this way.

She had given up hope completely when one day, in the computer lab, she checked her e-mail and found a message from

Sito@msc.uchicago.ed
Re: Seeking A Family Member

Sito? The name surprised her. The sender was from the University of Chicago. *Oh, yes, it must be Sheng Sito!* She recalled her visit to Chicago the year before.

***

She waited at Number 895 of a two-storey brick house. When the door opened, a young man with a brush cut stretched out his head and asked, "Yes. Can I help you?"

"I'm Xiaoyan's friend from Canada."

"Oh. She's not back yet. Come on in and have a seat," said the man.

Suyun thanked him and entered. She followed him into the living room and made herself comfortable on the couch.

"How did you get here, by taxi?"

"No. I took the subway and then two buses."

The man's eyes widened. "You are bold! I've lived here for eleven years, and have never dared to take the subway alone. I'm too afraid of robbers." He shook his head and grinned at her, incredulous.

"Robbers? Are you serious? I seldom hear about any robberies in St. John's."

"You country girl. Take a walk around the University of Chicago in the evening and you will find one in no time! And if you can't find any, I'll fetch one for you."

"You're kidding, right?" Suyun thought he was teasing her. He reminded her of someone, but she could not put her finger on whom. *Who does he resemble?* "Are you Taiwanese?" she asked.

"Why do you think I might be Taiwanese?"

"Well, you seem to have the same sense of loneliness and also the expectation that people from that island have."

"You have a sharp tongue, like the well-known Taiwanese journalist, Yingtai Long. She is an acute observer."

"After two years in Newfoundland, I've learned a lot about living on an island. Of course, an island in the Atlantic is not as hot as one in the Pacific."

"Ha! A genuine islander meets a fake one."

Suyun laughed. They shared the same kind of straightforward attitude when speaking.

"Hey!" Suyun's friend rushed into the living room, breathless but smiling. She embraced Suyun, and then stepped back to make the introductions. "Sheng, this is my former classmate, Suyun; and Suyun, this is my housemate, Sheng Sito."

"We have been getting to know each other," Suyun and Sheng smiled, answering in unison.

After a pleasant week's visit, Suyun left Chicago and returned to Newfoundland.

***

She was right. The message was from Sheng.

> *Dear Suyun Ren,*
>
> *I read your posting. We met in Chicago last year. I was very surprised to read your post. My father is Xianlin Ren. That would make him your uncle! And us cousins if we can find more evidence.*
>
> *I phoned my father who promised to send me a letter about his family history. If we are family though, I don't understand why you are from Xinjiang Province (you mentioned it when you were here). My father is from Guangdong Province. Hope you can tell me more about your family.*
>
> *By the way, my surname is after my mother.*
>
> *Hope things are fine with you.*
>
> *My best,*
>
> *Sheng Sito*

The words on the screen seemed to jump up and down in front of Suyun's eyes. She responded immediately.

June 25, 1996
Dear Sheng,

It's incredible to get in touch with you via the Internet. What you said in your message astounds me.

My father was born in Sichuan Province, and I, in Xinjiang Province. I don't know if his province of origin is Guangdong. I'll ask him. Father never mentioned his family to me in the past. I didn't know anything about the death of my grandparents or my uncle's disappearance until two weeks ago. My grandfather is Shenyu Ren (I have to ask my father about my grandmother's name). You could ask your father if your grandfather has the same name as my grandfather.

Please send me your mailing address. Then I can send you a photocopy of my father's letter.

It's difficult to make things any clearer right now.

Keep in touch and talk to you again soon.

Suyun

That same night, after much hesitation, she dialled the number of her father's factory.

"Hello, could you connect me with the benchwork workshop?"

"Who's calling?" asked the operator.

"Suyun," she answered with hesitation. "I would like to speak with my father, Xianpu Ren."

"I guessed it was you! We seldom receive long distance calls from overseas. I'll put you through to him."

She heard someone else pick up the receiver, Suyun asked, "May I speak to Master Ren?"

"Who's this?"

"Suyun."

"It's you! I didn't even recognize your voice." The speaker's voice sounded excited. "Are you calling from overseas? I'll get your father right away."

A few minutes later she finally heard her father ask, "Is anything urgent?" the worry in his voice palpable .

"Father, everything is okay. I have good news for you. I think I might've found Xianlin Ren."

"My heavens! Really? Where is he?"

"In Taiwan. One of his sons is in the States…"

"Is it possible?" Her father lowered his voice. "So many people in the world have the same name."

"What's my grandmother's name? Can you find a photo or anything left by your parents and brother?"

"Her name was Chunhua Ren-Zhang," he said, his voice almost a whisper. Her father then abruptly changed the topic. "Are you busy with your studies? I'll send you a letter very soon."

Immediately, Suyun realized it was not convenient for her father to talk about the family history over the phone. "My studies are going well. You take care, Father. I'll send you a registered letter."

The following day, she mailed a letter to her father. Then she received another e-mail message from Sheng.

From then on, the lives of the two brothers, unknown to each other for forty-six years, were suddenly connected by messages. Via truck, train, airplane, telephone, and computer, the messages crisscrossed between Xinjiang Province and Newfoundland, between Taipei and Chicago, and between Chicago and St. John's, as they traced the brothers' family history.

A month later, Suyun's father and Sheng's father finally held each other's photograph and heard each other's voices over the phone. Though the faces in the photographs appeared different from those remembered four decades ago, their voices were still recognizable. Exhilarated, they looked forward to a meeting in person.

In mid-August, Suyun passed the defence for her thesis. As planned, she would return to Wulumuqi City where her fiancé had been waiting for her for three years. A journalist position also awaited her. She and her cousin, Sheng, arranged for a family gathering. Suyun would join their fathers at Sheng's home in Chicago and then go back to China with her father on the same flight.

Patricia had a farewell party for Suyun and decorated her living room with strings of colourful balloons. At the sight of these balloons, Suyun thought, *I'll hang up all kinds of balloons at Sheng's home to celebrate the reunion of my father and his brother.* Delighted at the imagined meeting, she bought a large package of brightly coloured balloons.

By early September, Suyun was ready to leave. Patricia saw her off at the airport. "Have a good trip and a happy family reunion. Write to me from China."

"For sure. You have my word. Please send me a copy of your book when it's published," replied Suyun.

"Definitely." Patricia hugged her and said, "and don't forget to let me know the date of your wedding."

When Suyun thought about rejoining her fiancé, her eyes beamed. "Yes, I will."

She followed the crowd through the gate, and stepped into the passenger compartment. The plane rose slowly into the sky. She looked out the window from her seat. Clouds in different shapes drifted in the sunshine. Some appeared to take on human form and others seemed to be horses running across the blue sky. Newfoundland was shaped like an enormous leaf floating on the waves of the Atlantic Ocean, slowly becoming smaller and smaller. *Farewell, St. John's.* Suyun's eyes misted. On this lovely island three years had flown away like a black swallow swiftly dissolving into white clouds.

***

Several hours later, this large metal bird finally landed at O'Hare International Airport. The bright clouds were rising higher while a few other metal birds were landing on their own nests.

Exiting Customs, she spotted a woman with a little girl of five. She recognized them immediately from the photo Sheng had sent her. It was Sheng's wife, Fen, and their daughter. But she did not see Sheng and wondered where he was. When they finally stood facing one another, Suyun shook Fen's hand. "Where is Sheng?" she asked. Suddenly sensing something was wrong, she searched Fen's face for an answer. The little girl, standing beside Fen, gripped the strings of two helium-filled balloons, one white and the other black. The balloons tried to escape from the little girl's hand.

Fen's eyes were heavy. "He … he's…," she stammered.

"My daddy's gone to Taipei. He left this morning," said the little girl.

"Why?" She held her breath and looked into Fen's eyes, puzzled.

"My father-in-law, your uncle –" Fen stopped, tears streaming down her face. She took a deep breath. "Yesterday … we got a phone call from Sheng's brother, telling us my father-in-law had a heart attack before he boarded the plane. They sent him to the hospital right away, but he never regained consciousness and passed away."

Fen's story took Suyun aback. Shaking, she leaned against the railing, her hand grasping the bar, and her eyes fixed on the balloons held in the little girl's hand. When the little girl saw Suyun's despairing eyes, she could not help but call out, "Auntie-cousin!" She walked up to Suyun, and reached out to grab her hand. Unexpectedly, the balloons slipped from the girl's hand and bounced up to the ceiling. The white balloon became lodged against a light fixture. Suyun's eyes followed the black balloon that tumbled across the ceiling toward the other end of the hallway disappearing from view.

Fen wrapped her arm around Suyun's shoulder and rocked her gently. "Let's go to pick up your father. His plane arrives at a different gate. He'll be here in half an hour."

Suyun finally withdrew her gaze from the lost balloons and checked her watch. It read 7:18. *What will I tell my father?* She shuddered. "Yes, let's go," Suyun said, unable to hold back her tears. "I think we shouldn't mention my uncle's death to my father for the time being."

"Right," Fen said. "We could say he's postponed his trip because of some medical problem. Later, we'll tell him the truth."

Suyun nodded. Her mind's eye drifted: A young journalist for the *Central Daily* of the Nationalists in Guangzhou City fled to Taiwan after the Communists' takeover in 1949. The lanky man stood alone on the windy shore, staring in the distance over the South China Sea. He gripped in his hand a few letters that he had sent to Chongqing that were rejected at the border of China. The dictator's black hand had made China a birdcage wrapped in red flags. Thirty years later, after the door of this huge cage was opened, the middle-aged journalist sent more letters. But they returned with different stamps – the one to his parents stamped with the word "deceased," and the other to his younger brother with the word "disappeared."

Suyun envisioned these caged birds as wounded or lying belly-up. Many were now learning how to fly, but some had become colour-blind after having seen only the colour red throughout their lives. She cried in her heart: *My never-seen uncle, please rest in peace. You were lucky to have been free long before the other caged birds ever had a chance to see the sky.* The two women and the child exited the building and made their way through the airport to the international terminal. Suyun took a deep breath and looked up into the sky.

The sun, glittering like a gigantic, orange balloon, gradually dropped behind the city buildings. The world in front of Suyun blossomed into sunset. She was ready to greet her father.

*From "Report on an Investigation of the Peasant Movement in Hunan" (March 1927), Mao's *Selected Works*, Vol. I, p. 28.

TWIN RIVERS

IN HER BRA AND PANTIES, she ran along the bank of the St. Lawrence River. Footprint by footprint, one deep, the other shallow. Her left leg became heavy. The river reflected a sad, white glare in the sunset. Several blonde men and women in colourful bathing suits played in the ankle-deep water. Their cheerful splashes and voices echoed along the beach. Nobody noticed that a half-naked Chinese girl filled with shame was desperately chasing a man. The man had been her lover, but he deserted her after stripping her of her clothes. Unable to keep up with him, she burst into tears.

Jiang woke up, weeping. Her tears soaked her pillowcase. Her cozy bedroom seemed empty in the dark. Silvery moonlight slowly streamed in through the window and outlined her pale cheeks and puffy eyes.

The night before, she had dropped by Limin's apartment again. *Knock! Knock! Knock!* No one answered the door, but she could hear noises coming from inside. *He must be watching TV*, she thought. Anger spurted in her, and she kicked the door so hard that it finally opened.

A man in his late thirties stood near the door. He did not look at her when she entered. Instead, he shook his head as he turned and strode back to his seat. The television was on. On the coffee table lay a bottle of beer, and an empty can of pork with mustard leaf pickles. Jiang knew Limin would have also eaten a piece of apple pie or a Mae West cake. He enjoyed Chinese food combined with a western-style dessert.

"Why are you here again?" he asked, refusing to look at her.

"You must make a clear commitment to me!" Jiang shouted.

"I've already told you I'm unreliable." Limin shrugged. He was short, with round shoulders. Shrugging made him look funny. "Forgive me. You'll find a better man."

Listening to his pitiful tone, Jiang felt a twinge of sympathy for him. But when she visualized losing the only man in her life and remembered her lonely past, desperation filled her.

She glimpsed at the framed portrait of Limin and his wife that he had just recently displayed on the table. They looked as if they were grinning directly at her. Jiang even recognized the smirk that glared out of the photo. Her face clouded over with anger, as she grabbed the frame and flung it onto the floor. "If you don't marry me, death is the only way out!" Her voice sounded like the cracked glass from the frame shattering into tiny pieces. Limin gaped at the bits of scattered glass, then at her. She slammed the door shut on her way out.

After her nightmare, Jiang was unable to sleep.

***

Jiang had not found a boyfriend because of her lame leg. She was convinced of this. Many Chinese women her age – thirty-five – had by now become wives and mothers.

Years ago, when she was a student, she thought she had a chance at love. Once, she went to a student dance. She was so nervous about it that she had practiced dancing with one of her friends for weeks before the event, perfecting every movement, working hard at disguising her limp.

That night, a male student invited her to dance. Nervously, she joined him. They waltzed. She concentrated hard on following him, raising her left foot often to compensate for her limp. She did well. Looking at her partner's smiling face, she felt happier than she had been in long, long time. *Practice helps me, I can dance well!* She was grateful for her girlfriend who had practiced with her and encouraged her to come to the dance.

The young man seemed interested in her. He suggested they take a walk outside. He led her to a path flanked by gardens behind the dance hall. The heady scent of flowers mingled with the night breeze elated her. She felt confident. When he turned his head, she was startled to see that he had noticed her clumsy gait. "Did you hurt your leg while we danced?" he asked politely.

"No. I ... I enjoyed the dance," Jiang hesitated to explain. "I had polio as a child."

The young man seemed frozen for a second. "Is that true?" he said, his hand brushing the hair off his forehead. "Why don't I get you something to drink," he added. He made his way quickly to a vendor selling bottled juice on the sidewalk, as if he had fled from a corpse.

When he returned, he passed the juice to her. "Let's go back." Without waiting for Jiang's response, he strode purposely back to the dance hall.

Jiang's heart sank. She felt certain that her lame leg was the reason for his sudden change of heart. In China, a disability could mark you for life.

In Canada, she had hoped things would be different. She worked as a civil engineer after graduating from a Master's program at Queen's University in Kingston. On weekends, she liked to go to the university library's reading room to pour over newspapers and magazines in Chinese. She enjoyed reading in Chinese as it helped release in her the mixed feelings she had about living alone, studying hard, and striving to succeed in a new country without any relatives or close friends to turn to.

One afternoon, while immersed in a copy of *Readers* magazine, Jiang was interrupted by a male voice. "Excuse me, is that Issue Eight?"

She raised her head. "Yes, it is."

"Are you a student?"

"Just graduated. How about you?"

"Post-doctoral."

"Interesting." Jiang was curious. "Where did you get your Ph.D.?"

"London University."

"Wow!" she said, "You've been to England!"

They got along immediately. Limin looked modest and amiable, which made a good impression on Jiang.

They discovered they had, at one time, lived in the same province in China. Sharing their memories of the well-known local foods of Jiangsu Province made conversation easy. They recalled delicacies like the dry bean curd strips of Zhengjiang, the mini steamed buns stuffed with crab ova of Yangzhou, and the salted duck and boiled hatched eggs of Nanjing.

In time, they became more intimate with each other, going out to Chinese restaurants and watching movies several times a month. Considerate of her lame leg, Limin slowed down his step to match hers whenever they walked somewhere together. This flattered Jiang. Her experience told her that most Chinese men were more likely to avoid her after noticing her difference. It wasn't long before they began to spend nights together.

Jiang soon learned Limin had a wife and son in China. He hadn't tried to hide that. But he had never mentioned that they would come to Canada to join him either. She felt certain that he would choose her as his life partner and that together they would start a new life in this new country.

Then, two weeks ago, very suddenly, he announced, "The arrangements for my wife and child are done."

"What arrangements?" Her voice quivered. "Do you mean they're coming to Canada?"

"Of course." He looked at her and added, "We will have to stop; they'll be here soon."

She cleared her throat. "But what about our future?"

"We do not have a future. Why would you think this?"

"What?" She choked up and her lips trembled. "I didn't expect this."

"I told you I was married. This was pleasant. Love between a man and a woman benefits both," he said with a carefree tone. "Neither should blame the other when the time comes to part company."

She could not believe what she was hearing. They had been lovers for seven months. To her, a girl only lost her virginity to a man who would be her husband. She had played the role of wife for half a year. She knit wool sweaters for him, and he celebrated her birthday with her. He bought her gifts, and told her he cared about her. He had given her the impression that he had been comparing her to his wife in order to determine who would be a better life partner. She had been confident about her candidacy. She thought someday he would divorce his wife and marry her.

She could not believe their love affair had come to an end. That's why she went to see him, to confront him. He had to make a commitment. He owed it to her.

***

The morning sun rose gradually, but she could not see any signs of hope with this new day. She needed a shoulder to cry on, but did not have any friends or relatives to whom she could pour out her sad story. She thought of her father and how much she missed him. At that moment her father's death came back to haunt her like a nightmare relived. Her eyes dimmed with dismay as if she had seen dead water slowly flooding the world.

She heard a knock on the door. When the second knock sounded, she got out of bed and threw on some clothes, wondering who could be knocking at this hour. *Is it him?*

"Ms. Jiang Liu, open the door! It's the police."

She was astonished. Why had the police come? She hurried out of the bedroom and rushed to open the front door. Two constables entered the living room, a man and a woman. The policewoman asked, "Is your name Jiang Liu?"

Jiang nodded.

"Last night did you drop by Mr. Limin Ding's place?"

"Yes."

"Did you damage anything?"

"We—"

"Threaten him with death?"

"I—I was angry." Jiang had not expected Limin to report the incident to the police.

"So," the policewoman continued, "we assume Mr. Ding told us the facts, unless you deny what happened. This is a warning. You harass Mr. Ding again, and he complains, we will have to lay charges."

Jiang's face turned ashen. The policewoman handed her a business card. "Ms. Liu," she said sympathetically, "give me a call if you need help. But please, for your own sake, don't phone or visit Mr. Ding again. Do you understand?"

"Yes, of course." Jiang nodded. She gazed into the policewoman's young, kind face, then pleaded with her own. "But, you don't understand...."

"Understand what?" The two constables waited for a moment. But Jiang did not say anything more.

Dizzy and exhausted, Jiang returned to the bedroom after the police left. She lay down and buried her face in her pillow. She did not have the energy to get ready to go to work. She would stay home.

***

Jiang was named after the Yangtze River. She was born into a teacher's family. Her father taught mathematics at a secondary school, and her mother taught Chinese history at an elementary school. As a child, Jiang's lame leg didn't seem to matter as she came from a loving and caring family.

In the early summer of 1966, with the arrival of the Cultural Revolution, everything changed. At that moment, the entire world became chaotic and it seemed that everybody was riled up, and afraid.

One day, her father found a half page of *The People's Daily* with Chairman Mao's portrait on the dirty floor in a public washroom. He picked up the page, took it home, and then burned it as he did not like to see Mao's portrait sullied. Her mother saw him burning Mao's image and reported it to the "Rebels" organization at the secondary school. The revolutionists arrested her father and shaved one side of his head, giving him a yin-yang head – a form of humiliation enacted on anti-revolutionaries. Then they forced him to kneel down and confess his crime at a denunciation meeting. Unable to endure torture and fearing a jail sentence, her father drowned himself.

Heartbroken, Jiang abhorred her mother and hated the Cultural Revolution, but dared not speak out. She was no longer a cheerful stream, but a long, dark river, running to nowhere.

***

It was past two o'clock when she woke up with an empty stomach.

She went to the kitchen, took some food from the fridge, and fixed herself a meal: plain rice, prawns with sweet and sour sauce, and soup with greens and a shredded egg. She ate, but it tasted like nothing. All she could think about was Limin, and how he had betrayed her. After the meal, she picked up a small hammer and threw it into her handbag. She went to her car and drove to Limin's apartment. She made sure to park about a block away.

It was a pleasant afternoon and many people were out strolling along the riverbank. Jiang felt as though she were floating through the quiet streets as she walked toward a gracious older house that had been turned into several different units. Upon arriving, she climbed up the exposed stairs, clutching her handbag. She reached the second-floor balcony and knocked on the door. Nobody answered, just as she expected. She reached into her handbag and drew out the hammer, then slammed it against the window next to the door. The glass fell with a crash, and then the door of Limin's apartment opened. She stepped in and screamed, "I'm here for you to call the police!" she shouted, wildly brandishing her hammer, then flinging it at the television screen when she saw Limin's face cringe. Without saying a word, Limin dialled for the police.

Jiang fell into the armchair and cried like a baby. A few minutes later, a police car stopped at the building. Two officers came to take her away.

***

Sleeplessness caused Jiang's memory to constantly shift into the past, back to her life in China. She worked at the Provincial Institute of Science and Technology after graduating from the university. She expected to meet her Mister Right, but there were only two young men at the institute who would give her the time of day. And yet, when she would talk to either man, he either indicated he did not have the time to speak or he said he had a meeting to attend. Her female colleagues introduced her to a couple of men, but they never showed interest in her, probably because of her lame leg she thought.

Once, at work, she discovered some flaws in a building plan submit-ted by a factory and helped correct them. Afterwards, she received a phone call from the designer who wanted to speak to the person who had improved his design. When Jiang had said, "Speaking," the man she had been speaking to was suddenly silent. "I did that work," she repeated. "I'm Jiang Liu. Is something wrong?" she asked.

"I thought," he stammered. "I … I didn't expect a woman, a young woman." She could sense his smirk over the phone line. "I am sorry for the misunderstanding."

"Do you think a young woman cannot read the building plan?" Jiang teased.

"No, no. I mean I'm very glad to know you. Thanks for your help. Do you mind if I call you and ask for your help again? By the way, I'm Wenlong."

After that Wenlong had called more often. Sometimes they chatted on the phone about other things besides business. They discovered they were both single and they both enjoyed talking to each other. One day, deliberately, Jiang mentioned the story of Zhang Haidi, whom she had read about earlier that year. It was a story about a girl who had become confined to a wheelchair, but who had struggled to achieve all her goals, despite the obstacles she had had to face because of her disability. She was delighted when Wenlong told her he admired Zhang Haidi very much. So when Wenlong suggested they finally meet in person, Jiang accepted.

They arranged to meet in a restaurant downtown. Jiang arrived feeling somewhat apprehensive. She chose a cozy table in a dimly lit corner. Wenlong entered the restaurant shortly after work, carrying a beautiful pink rose in his hand. When he handed her the rose Jiang felt her face flush hot, an irrepressible smile on her lips.

They ate and chatted amicably about all kinds of things. Her heart was full, and happy. *I finally found a man who cares about me! How lucky I am!*

It was only after their meal, as they left the restaurant, that Wenlong noticed her limp. "I'm very sorry," he said, looking at her quizzically.

"What are you sorry about?" Jiang asked, trying to understand what seemed to trouble him.

"I didn't know –," Wenlong said as he escorted her to the bus stop. His eyes looked confused.

"About my leg?" she asked. Now Jiang was confused. "But, you said you admired Zhang Haidi. I didn't think my leg would be an issue," Jiang added, eyes downcast.

"Sorry," was Wenlong's only parting word as he hurriedly walked away from the stop, leaving her alone to wait for the bus.

Eventually, almost all of her female friends either had boyfriends or were married. She was alone and had more time than them. She began to bury herself in studies, in preparation for the English language test she had to take as part of her admission into a North American university. She passed and was finally accepted into a graduate program.

Before leaving for Kingston, Canada, she returned to her hometown of Wuhan City to visit her mother. Her mother had lived a lonely life since her father's death. Jiang was finally able to forgive her mother for what she had done to her father, recognizing that in those years, most of the people had been brainwashed and fooled by Mao's revolution. Her mother had not wanted to remarry though she had had many suitors. She told Jiang she had paid the price for her stupidity, adding, "If you find a suitable man, don't lose him."

Jiang mulled over what her mother had said before she left China. She had thought Limin was a suitable man. Now all she wanted was revenge; she wanted to pour out all her hot anger. She did not realize that in Canada, women had more choices. A woman could remain single and be happy. A woman could adopt a child or live with another woman to form her family. This was not real for Jiang. All Jiang could feel was her shame and humiliation. She was bitterly aware that Limin had used her. He had taken her virginity from her without ever intending to marry her. He had led her to believe he cared for her, despite her lame leg. She thought she had found in Canada what she had been denied in China. He had made a fool of her, and now he was using the law in Canada to dispose of her. He had taken her honour, and her dignity. It was unforgivable and intolerable. The shame and pain she felt was as intense as when her father had taken his life, abandoning her to a mother that had done the unthinkable and with whom she would never feel safe again.

***

When it was time for her to go to court, Jiang appeared at the hearing looking haggard and defeated. Standing still, she stared blindly at the audience in front of her and admitted she had been harassing Limin.

At last the judge announced, "Jiang Liu is convicted of the charge of repeated harassment. You are hereby sentenced to serve 90 days in jail and are fined $1,000. Because you have no criminal record, you are to be placed on probation for one year." The judge made a final warning: "You must stay away from Mr. Limin Ding. A breach of this court order will result in a jail sentence."

Home from court, inflamed with anger and shame, Jiang kicked off her shoes, sat on the bed and punched her pillow. She had never expected she would land up in court. The phrase "jail sentence" haunted her. So afraid of life in jail, her father had killed himself years before. She was only seven when he died. She pictured a corpse floating in the dirty water of the city moat, its swollen face half-covered by grass and fallen leaves. The body was identified as her father's. The "anti-revolutionary" had destroyed himself before others could.

She wept bitterly. She imagined Limin and his wife holding wine glasses to celebrate their reunion. He would lie to her and tell her that he loved her. *He thinks he's a lady-killer. But he is nothing more than a cheater who plays with women.* Jiang determined that she would let his wife know he had been unfaithful. Suddenly, she got up and pulled open her drawers and closet to collect all the gifts she had received from Limin: a pair of earrings, two dresses, and a model of a Victorian-style building. After she had stuffed all of the items into her tote bag, she clenched her fist tightly. She imagined throwing all of his gifts in his face, and could almost feel her pain being released.

She knew doing this meant jail. But it didn't matter. Revenge fully occupied her mind. She wanted Limin to know what humiliation and shame was like. Jiang did not understand why it was she who was being punished. He was the one who should suffer.

She picked up her tote bag and hurried to her car. She got behind the wheel, pressed her foot on the gas and rushed away.

Once more, she banged on Limin's door, and once again, he had to open the door. She flung her tote bag at him but Limin dodged, and the bag thudded against the floor. Its contents spilled out onto the tiles, the model house splitting in two. Jiang looked around and did not see anybody else in the apartment. She ran over to the tote bag, knelt down, and started pulling out clothes and jewellery to hurl at Limin.

He stepped back and picked up the telephone receiver as a dress landed on his shoulder and an earring clung to his hair. Limin rushed into the bathroom and locked himself in. His concentration was so focused on pressing the buttons on the phone that he did not even hear what she was shouting. The anger she felt inside overwhelmed her and poured out of her as she crashed about in the kitchen. After dialling, he sat on the floor and listened to her walking between the kitchen and his bedroom. Jiang was repeatedly filling a container with water and pouring it on the bed. She did this over and over again until Limin's double bed was flooded. Then she fell to the floor.

Ten minutes later, Limin heard sirens approaching the building. At a policeman's request, he opened the door and stepped out onto the balcony, almost tripping on the scattered items she had thrown on the floor.

The police arrested Jiang for a second time.

***

She was placed into a local jail for women. It was a one-storey building that looked like a motel, with a front lawn and garden surrounded by tall fir trees. It looked quite different from the provincial prison near her university campus in Nanjing. That prison had high walls and electric barbed wire. Its gate adjoined a post, where an armed soldier stood with a rifle. But here with the sun shining, and birds chirping, she did not find the place as terrifying. If only she could stop thinking, "jail." If only she were not handcuffed.

As soon as she walked into the structure and faced the walls, she felt depressed. In front was a reception room and on the left was a lounge for the staff. A door on the right led into a corridor with a wall on one side and rooms on the other. A female guard showed her the dining room, washing room and day room where inmates could play cards, watch TV, and read newspapers and magazines, such as *The Globe and Mail, Kingston This Week,* and *Chatelaine.*

"You can take walks in the corridor except during sleeping hours. Every day from 2:00 p.m. to 3:00 p.m. is free time outside of the building."

The guard led her to a cell. "Well, here you are. Any questions?"

"No," said Jiang as the guard locked her in. She saw a bed, a dresser, a chair, a sink, and a toilet. At that moment she realized she had lost her freedom.

In the cell, she opened her suitcase, took her things out and put them into the drawers of the tiny dresser next to the bed. With permission from the police, she had brought along tapes of Chinese songs and a cassette player. Suppertime arrived just after she had finished putting everything away. She left the cell and followed the others into the dining room. At her table, there were only three other women prisoners.

She took a plate with fries, boiled peas, carrots, and two pieces of ham. The others ate hamburgers with salad.

"Why you inside?" one of the women asked. She was large, with stringy blonde hair and a blank look.

Jiang did not realize the question was directed at her until a fork tapped on her plate. She answered reluctantly. "For harassment—"

"Huh!" another woman grinned. "Terrific!" She had large, dark eyes with bushy eyebrows. When she spoke, her red lips glistened, and the smirk on her face said nothing bothered her. "I'm Michelle. Got a sentence of thirty-five days for beating up my husband. I'll get a divorce when I'm out, in two days. He your boyfriend or ex?"

Jiang shook her head, not wanting to talk about it.

"Men are something bad. They harass you, you harass them back. Look here." She pulled up her left sleeve and pointed at a dark scar. "That rat stabbed me. He deserved what he got."

Chuckling, Michelle patted the shoulder of the older woman next to her, who didn't respond at all, her eyes empty. "This here is Rosa, a single mom. Got herself a little girl. Got herself a good education but no job. She tried to drown her daughter in the river, so she's got to go to court tomorrow."

"What happened?" Jiang gasped. "Why would she do such a thing?"

"Husband beat them both. Then he started touching the kid."

Jiang trembled. "What happened to her child?"

"Given to a guardian."

Lost in thought about Rosa's poor little girl, Jiang wondered what kind of future that child would have.

"Joan," Michelle had trouble pronouncing Jiang's name. "You do Tai Chi? Maybe if I know that, I can punch back…"

"Tai Chi is not like martial arts. It's just exercises."

"Is that right?" Michelle rolled her eyes.

Jiang nodded. "What would you have done if you were Rosa?" she asked out of curiosity.

"I'm not sure, but I wouldn't have taken the easy way out." Michelle looked hard at Jiang. "I would ask for help from a women's shelter."

Jiang returned to her cell after supper. She could not stop thinking about Rosa's daughter. She picked out a tape, and inserted it into the cassette slot and pressed the play key.

"I Want to Have My Own Home." This had been one of her favourite songs. It brought to mind her dream of the once sweet childhood home she had known before her father died.

After the Revolution ended with Mao's death in 1976, entrance examinations for university were re-established. Jiang passed the exams and had the opportunity to enroll in a university in a city far away from home. She never returned home.

Despite the awareness of her mother's profound regret, Jiang found it hard to be close to her mother. She had heard many such stories of betrayal that had happened between lovers, husbands and wives, siblings, children and parents. They had been told that to be a loyal revolutionary to Mao, one must sacrifice their own family members who had different opinions and/or who talked against Mao and the Communist Party. In her last year at university, her mother came to visit. She had developed insomnia, her pale and wrinkled face looking older than her actual age. Over and over, her mother repeated, "I did not realize, I did not realize…" Jiang found it hard to be sympathetic. After her father's death, her mother was dead to her, too. She felt like an orphan.

As the years went by, Jiang's youth slipped away. Like a brook, she flowed from the East to the West. To her, women needed husbands, just like rivers running into the sea. Her childhood home had included a husband, and then a child.

For Jiang, a woman without a husband was nothing.

***

She changed the tape after the first one stopped. Listening to the familiar Chinese music soothed her. Her sorrow blurred and receded. A deep voice resounded:

Stars move across the sky
The path shines under moonlight
The hill no longer looks high
Childhood vanishes from my sight

She sighed and thought: *Rosa's little girl will grow up and become an adult. Maybe she will forget what her mother tried to do to her.*

The Yangtze River joins the sea
I sail to another river
A question rises in me
Where is my harbour?

She could feel the yellow currents pushing against the Yangtze River as she listened to the song echoing in the room.

Later that night as she lay on her cot, listening to the thunder cracking in the sky, she envisioned a black swirl in the long, dark river through which a lonely sailboat passed. She tossed and turned. The following day, Jiang's head was heavy from a sleepless night. During the prisoners' free time outside, she walked into the surrounding gardens. When nobody was looking, she slipped into the back yard and jumped easily over the small, unguarded fence, not far from which was the St. Lawrence River. She trudged to the river and stepped into the shallow water. The sunlight danced on the surface, and the water felt warm to the touch. Shuffling along, she waded into the middle of the river. She thought she could see her father's face smiling then frowning. The river's currents swamped her legs, then her waist. The image of Rosa holding her daughter in the water flashed in her mind. When the currents reached her torso, she found it hard to hold herself up. The sound of the waves struck at her ears. She could hear Rosa's little girl crying. Michelle's words also resounded: "I wouldn't have taken the easy way out."

Hours later, Jiang awoke in a hospital bed. She could not help but laugh hysterically. Then she cried. In her mind only endless and soundless white waves pushed around her. Jiang's head spun, and her body shook. Then, she disappeared into the water.

HERBS

*Some herbs are robust. Snow Lotus can survive at −20°C to −30°C,
and Common Horsetail can root itself in the sand. I wish I were a
hardy herb.*

— An excerpt from Yan Tan's Diary

WITH PERPLEXED EYES, she looked out the window from her seat
on the plane. The clouds over the American Continent floated
up and down, just like her mixed thoughts. She massaged her forehead
as if she were trying to erase an unpleasant memory.

The plane bounced and landed on the runway at Boise Air Terminal
in Houston. Fast-moving passengers had already retrieved their carry-
on baggage and were ready to leave their seats, but Yan was reluctant
to give up the sense of freedom she had felt since the plane left China.
Just then, an idea flashed in her mind: *I'm free now; I can go wherever
I want!* Excited by the idea, she made a sudden decision not to go to
the International Language School in Houston that her husband had
insisted she attend. He'd said that if she learned to speak English better,
she would be able to help him more with his business. Just the thought
of it made her legs weak.

When the man next to her stood up and put the strap of a travel bag
over his shoulder, she smoothed her dress and rose, too. Taking her
suitcase from the overhead compartment, she followed the others and
left the plane with a new resolve.

When she lined up with a luggage cart at the Custom's exit, she detected a placard held by someone with Chinese characters: Yan Tan. She hastily turned her cart around and followed another crowd of arriving passengers out through another exit.

An airport coach waited outside the entrance of the hall. She approached it and asked the driver, "Excuse me, sir, does this bus go downtown?"

"Yes. Get in, please." Noticing she was alone, the driver stepped down from the bus to help load her luggage. She had no idea where she was going or what she was going to do. Sitting on the bus, she remembered reading about the city of New Orleans, its culture, diversity, and its beauty, which attracted an influx of tourists.

Two days later at the City Bank in New Orleans, in front of the service counter for new accounts, she filled out the application form, signed her name, and deposited all of her $2,000 into her new account, which had aptly been advertised as a "Freedom Chequing Account."

***

Yan strolled past Jackson Square where the gothic structure of St. Louis Cathedral towered over the Pontalba Apartments. She wandered along Saint Peter Street. Bright and scorching sunlight emitted heat around her, but a breeze from the Mississippi River blowing through the Square brought cool air. Her short hair bobbed slightly as she walked. Looking at the buildings along the sidewalk, she glimpsed ferns, vines, and blooming morning glory climbing up the cast iron banisters. Various handicrafts were displayed on sidewalk stands under the shade of trees. A thought occurred to her: *If I run out of money, I can do the same.* She felt exhilarated when she imagined herself selling the handicrafts she had brought with her as gifts: a dozen pure embroidered silk scarves, two sets of sculptures of camels and horses made of tri-coloured glazed clay in the Tang Dynasty style, and more than a dozen necklaces of carved bone beads packed in delicate brocade boxes.

She roamed the streets, all her senses focused on savouring the exotic atmosphere of the architecture, as well as the fragrance of cape honeysuckle, glory bower, and yellow cassia. Her excitement so overpowered her fatigue from the lengthy trip that she almost forgot her uncertainty in this new city.

Later, Yan arrived at the French Market where the vendors' stands full of various fruit attracted her. With delight, she looked over the exotic choices, some of which were unknown to her. She bought fresh figs, blueberries, raspberries, and blackberries. Then she touched a pale green, pear-shaped fruit and asked the vendor, "What's this?"

"Papaya," the young woman answered, smiling at her. "It tastes great; try it."

Yan bought one and also picked up a few kiwis.

She ate berries while she loitered about the market, the raspberries turning her lips and fingers bright red. Finally, she passed through the French Market and reached Le Café du Monde. Tourists in twos and threes were perched around the patio tables in the yard outside the café, appreciating the sunshine under umbrellas – umbrellas that looked as if large, white-and-blue striped mushrooms were blooming out of the concrete lawn. Yan asked for a café au lait and a beignet. Then, she found a seat and sat down.

Nearby, two singers sang cheerfully as they played guitars. In the distance, a girl and a boy of about eighteen, in T-shirts and shorts, loped toward the café. The girl walked ahead of the boy, then hid inside a doorway, one finger pointing at him. The boy pretended not to notice her finger and passed by the door. Then, with mock surprise, he turned his head and grasped her finger. Then he pulled the girl out from the doorway and kissed her. The girl walked ahead of the boy again and repeated her trick. They seemed to enjoy the game, like children indulging in hide-and-seek.

Watching them play prompted memories of her cousin. Yan looked out into the streets of New Orleans and saw another scene, from a decade earlier, unfold in front of her.

***

A teenaged girl stood on the bank of a brook running through Peach Blossom Valley and stared at the float on a fishing line. Unexpectedly a rain shower poured down. She collected her fishing rod and rushed toward a tree.

"Yan! It's dangerous to go under the tree," her cousin, Heng, called out. He was twenty-two, a senior student in the law program at the local university. Running up to her, he grasped her arm, "Let's get some cover over there."

They reached a giant protruding rock at the edge of the riverbank and took refuge under it. Heng stood close to the edge of the rock to keep the rain off Yan. She couldn't help but put her arms around his waist.

She was shivering, despite his warmth, so she dropped her hands and murmured, "Heng, I'm a little cold."

He turned to her and gently took hold of her shoulders, "It'll be sunny soon. You won't feel cold anymore."

Yan raised her head and noticed his broad chest trembling under his wet shirt. His eyes were bright and intelligent, and his chin sported a light beard. She realized that he was not only her childhood playmate but also an attractive man.

As a child, she used to ask him, "Be my friend forever?"

Heng always answered, "Of course, you puppy," with a smile, and then moved out of the way to avoid her fists.

She would yell, "I'm not a puppy!"

"Are you still cold?" Heng lowered his head and looked at her tenderly. A few raindrops from his hair dripped on her face; it tickled. When she put her hands on his chest, she could feel the rise and fall of his breath, the steady beat of his heart. He drew her close and felt her body melt against his, her breath quickening. Suddenly, he let her go. He paused for a moment and stepped back, then wiped the raindrops on her face with his finger. "The rain is over. Let's go home."

***

After finishing her café au lait and beignet, Yan left Le Café du Monde. She walked along a path through a garden and detected a familiar scent. Looking around the garden, she discovered many pineapple weeds, each stem carrying a yellowish flower on top. When Yan was a child, she and her playmates used to pluck handfuls of these sweet-scented flower heads and sew them into two-inch square ragbags. They would play with the bags; each player would throw the bag up in the air with her palm up, then she would flip her palm down and try to catch the bag with the back of her hand. After that she would add one more bag and try to catch one after the other on the back of her hand until the pile grew so high she can no longer steady all the weight and the bags fell to the ground. The girls named the plant "fragrant bag grass."

Yan had always taken an interest in herbs. At university she majored in Traditional Chinese Medicine, and studied herbs extensively. She had come across the real name of the fragrant bag grass—pineapple weed—by chance one afternoon in the university library while researching another herb. She was surprised and delighted, all these years later, to find the same grass in a garden in New Orleans. She still remembered the entry for pineapple weed in *The Illustrated Encyclopaedia of Herbs*:

"An annual herb, pineapple weed is probably a native of north-east Asia but it became established in North America before the nineteenth century. The cone-shaped flower head is yellow-greenish with a strong pineapple or apple scent when crushed. The flower heads are used medicinally."

In the garden outside Le Café du Monde, she plucked a pineapple weed flower. Its scent reminded her of her childhood and of her student life. A few salty drops touched her lips. She was not sure whether it was tears or sweat. Yan wiped her face with her hand as she raised her head. Watching people walk around, the sun hot on her face and shoulders, and hearing the different languages, she realized that she was alone in a remote country.

***

Several weeks later, Yan found a job at a grocery store named Saigon Village. The storeowner was Chinese-Vietnamese. He had escaped from North Vietnam more than two decades earlier. She also found a small, furnished apartment that was near the store, so she could walk to work every day. In her diary she wrote: "I've travelled a long way to a faraway place, and never expected in America I would meet people from Vietnam who speak Chinese."

Yan worked as a cashier and also helped clean the shelves and put away goods. She was pleased to discover that the storeowner subscribed to a Chinese newspaper, *The World Journal*. When she had some free time she borrowed the paper and enjoyed reading Chinese. One day, after she finished reading the current issue, she skimmed through a pile of back issues.

In the August 30 paper she found a "Seeking-Person" note: "Female: Yan Tan, 28, from Wenzhou City, China, is missing after her arrival at Houston Airport on August 16. If anyone has any information about Yan Tan, please call Mrs. Lee collect at (713) 555-4444. Reward offered."

Mrs. Lee was a business friend of her husband, Han Huang. Lee had arranged for Yan's arrival and also for her accommodation in Houston. Yan imagined her husband's shock when the Lee family informed him that she had never arrived. Vanishing was her ticket to freedom, the only choice she had to end her two-year nightmare.

***

On a Saturday evening two years earlier, Yan's husband asked her to go dancing with him.

At the dance hall, he pointed at a man and said, "That's Wu, the owner of the hall. He earns more than a hundred thousand yuan a month." Han added, "Tonight, nobody's going to leave without having fun. Yan, you should enjoy yourself too; don't be a party pooper."

"Party pooper? That depends on whether I like it or not."

"You won't know if you don't try." Han held her waist and pulled her to the dance floor. "Come on."

During a musical lull, they sat at a table sipping the drinks a young man had brought to the table on a silver tray.

"What is this?" Yan asked, delicately holding her glass and staring into it. "The green looks so pretty and the cherry inside is inviting."

"You mean the drink? This is a Grasshopper. It's a cocktail." Han winked and smiled. "I bet you'll want another one."

"I do like it," she said, smiling at her husband.

An older man who had been watching them from across the room approached the table and invited Yan to dance. Han patted her hand and encouraged her to accept. "Have fun," he said, his smile broad. "I'll find another partner."

Yan followed the man onto the dance floor and moved in time with the music. She looked at her dancing partner, who was in his late forties and in a good shape. He was an excellent dancer and Yan did her best to follow him gracefully. After several dances, she felt dizzy and sweaty. The man's hand had caressed her back, and his moustache sometimes touched her face. This made her uncomfortable, and she shivered, goose bumps spreading all over her body.

"Let's take a break," said Yan, "I'm tired."

As soon as she left him, another man appeared before her. "Yan, how about dancing with me?" he asked, his arm outstretched, inviting her.

"How do you know my name?" she asked, puzzled by his seeming familiarity.

"I'm your husband's friend, so I know your name."

Oh, it's Wu, she thought, remembering what Han had told her about him earlier. He was one of her husband's business associates. Han had mentioned they might run into him. She touched his hands with a tentative smile. He looked like he was in his mid-forties. His many wrinkles made his face look like petals when he smiled. Pulling her up towards him, his large hands then encircled her waist with ease. "So, you're Han's woman –"

"Pardon me?"

"I mean, you're Han's wife."

They waltzed. Wu held her gently. His breath blew a little on her face as he said, "You're a great dancer. Do you dance often?"

"Often? No," she answered. "I used to dance as a student." She had accepted another drink and now felt excited, not herself. Her feet moved to the rhythm of the music as though she were walking on clouds.

"If you like, you can come here to dance anytime."

"Anytime? I don't know if I have the time," replied Yan. Her forehead was almost resting on his chin. Out of the corner of her eye, she noticed that several dancing couples were kissing each other. She was shaken and tried to keep a certain distance from Wu, but he kept pulling her closer, so that their cheeks almost touched.

"What are you afraid of?" Wu tilted his head and chuckled. "It's a cheek-to-cheek dance. Don't you like it?"

"Yes, yes, I do," she said, her body relaxing against his, ignoring the warning signals firing off in her mind.

"Oh! You're graceful," he said, his lips lightly brushing her face and then her lips.

A few minutes later, Yan was being dragged into a room.

When she awoke, she was naked in a strange bed. A hand was draped across her breasts. It took some time before she realized that it was Wu who lay next to her. Suddenly she remembered the dance they shared earlier that evening. She bolted upright and scanned the room for her clothes. Wu must have heard her because he woke up abruptly and pulled her forcefully back down to the bed. "Don't dash off. You're mine tonight," he said, his lips stretched in an unsettling leer.

"Go to hell!" she screamed, trying desperately to push him away. But he was stronger than she was. With a callous laugh, he easily pinned her down. "I'll call the police!" she shouted, the dread in her voice palpable.

"Call the police? I didn't force you to join me."

"Han will beat you," she gasped, trying to control the panic that was welling up inside her.

"Ha!" Wu's breath was shallow and fast. His body pushed up against hers, forcing her open. "He consented!"

Shocked and numb, she felt herself droop in Wu's arms.

"Han has lots of women," Wu snickered, his mouth finding her neck.

"Lots of women? Impossible. He loves me." Yan felt a knife slice through her heart.

"I'm sure he does. But he likes to hang out with other women whenever he goes on a trip, and sometimes even when he's home." Wu's weight against her was unbearable.

"Leave me alone! Please," she pleaded, tears coursing down her cheeks.

"No, no. We are part of the sexual revolution." Wu maintained control over her body, pushing harder, hurting her. "Let yourself go. Have some fun. Han's doing the same thing I am now."

When he finally spent himself inside her, Yan felt as though she had fallen through the earth, buried under mounds of dirt, struggling to breathe. She crawled into herself, small and insignificant.

The next morning, Wu finally let her go, and she returned home, uncertain of what to expect. When she entered the living room, she was surprised to find Han relaxing on the couch and sipping tea as though nothing had happened.

"Did you have a good time?"

"Good time? How dare you?" she screamed. "So, this is your disgusting secret?"

"So? You did the same thing I did. We're a modern couple," he said, his smile mocking her.

"I was drugged; you're corrupted. I can't believe you did this to me. I'm leaving! I want a divorce. I want out right now," she stammered, unable to hold back the flood of tears that scalded her cheeks.

"Why?" he asked, looking up at her. "Didn't you enjoy it? Come on, admit it," he said, pulling her toward him, his hands running over her breasts.

"You're disgusting," she said, pushing him away with a vehemence she didn't know she had.

"Disgusting? You just don't know how to enjoy sexual freedom. Everybody around the world wants this, and you can have it. And your husband doesn't mind."

"After our divorce, you can enjoy your sexual freedom," she sputtered, her heart pounding wildly. She could not believe what she was hearing. Her head was spinning.

"But I don't want a divorce," he said, his voice cold.

"Why not?" she asked, trying not to shudder.

"You're a good wife. I need you, and you need me, too. I don't think you can find a husband more capable than me. And you will do as I say."

That's when she slapped him across the face, hard.

In her diary, she wrote: "I will never forget or forgive Han for what he has done to me. There are no herbs that can heal a bleeding heart." Then she tore the page into pieces. She did not have anywhere to go.

***

A bunch of green shrubs grew in a small garden in the yard of Saigon Village. The wife of the storeowner called them a "soup vegetable." One day, she handed Yan a basket and a pair of scissors and asked, "Can you cut off some soup vegetable for me?"

"How do you want me to do it?"

"Just snip off the leaves. No stems."

Yan went to the shrubs in the corner of the yard and gently fingered the shrub's shiny, oval leaves that smelled of a familiar herb – the wolfberry. She remembered the large wolfberry shrub in her grandmother's backyard. In the early fall, the shrub would be full of wolfberries that she called "doggy teeth." She would eat the shrub's tiny golden-orange fruit, savouring their sweet and sour taste. She had not known that its leaves were also edible.

She felt homesick as she cut the leaves off the thorny branches. She hadn't written to her parents, sister, or brother because she did not want Han to trace her. *Do they think I'm dead?* she asked herself. *Maybe I am dead.*

When she returned the basket full of wolfberry leaves to the store-owner's wife, Yan asked politely, "Is this an American wolfberry shrub?"

"Wolfberry?" the woman repeated. "I have no idea. This shrub originally came from China."

"When did you go to China?"

"Not me," sighed the woman. "It's a long story."

"Who brought it here?" Yan pressed, wanting to get to the bottom of the story.

"The wife of my husband's granduncle took it with her when she joined her husband in America. She died just after her arrival, but the shrub survived. My granduncle and his son always used its leaves to make their favourite soup. The shrub became like a family member, following them wherever and whenever they moved."

Yan imagined the wolfberry's new branches spreading as they moved with the family from California to New York, then to Rhode Island, to finally take root in the soil of New Orleans. The story of the shrub made her think about her situation. That night she wrote in her diary: "I know now I will never go back to Han. I came to America at his suggestion, to improve my English. Now I am here and free. Perhaps, I should plant my own roots in this country, just like the store owner's wolfberry shrub."

Weeks later, when she scanned *The World Journal*, another note caught her eye: "Yan, please contact me at (602) 555-4000. Heng."

That was the one name that could stir in her feelings of happiness, sadness, and longing. She had tried to forget him a long time ago, but any thought of him still made her weak, despite their many years apart. As she remembered her cousin, memories came flooding back.

***

After they went fishing for the last time, Heng seldom visited her home. Yan always found some excuse to go to her aunt's apartment. Whenever she saw him, her spirits soared. When she could not see him, she was lost, bereft. He always seemed happy to see her, but kept his distance.

After graduation, Heng found a job as a researcher in a law institute. From her aunt, Yan heard that many girls were interested in him, but he did not seem interested in anyone in particular, and that made his mother worry about him.

Yan became a university student a few years later but was never attracted to any of the young men she met there. Only the thought of Heng could rouse butterflies in her stomach. She knew that their families, their friends, and all of society, would not accept a romantic relationship between cousins. Yet, she could not stop herself from wondering whether he felt the same affection for her.

Two years slipped away. She heard one day that he intended to pursue further education in the United States. She felt as though her heart had become a dead weight inside her. Knowing he would be far away and difficult to see again, Yan decided she needed to see him for one last time to say farewell.

She arrived at his dormitory room on a grey and rainy afternoon. Cardboard boxes and suitcases cluttered the floor. He led her into the only armchair in the room, and he sat on his bed.

"All done?"

"Yes." He sounded tired.

"So, you are leaving," was the only thing she managed to say, her eyes fixed on the dandelions that decorated a mug on the table. Her thoughts wafted in the air like the dandelion's seeds. She had a lot to say, but said nothing. Not able to hold back her tears, she turned her face aside. She did not want him to see her cry.

"Please, don't cry," he said, coming over to her. He pulled a handkerchief out of his pocket, then knelt down. He wiped her tears away.

She grasped his hand and asked, "Why do you ignore me? What are you afraid of?"

"Aren't you afraid?" he answered, folding the handkerchief into a tiny square that he placed carefully on the coffee table behind him. "We're cousins."

"What if we don't want a child," she finally uttered.

"Don't be silly." Heng gently touched her hair and said, "We can't ignore our parents, and we can't ignore the laws or society. Can we?"

"Why not? We can live somewhere far away..."

"Yeah. Eat grass roots, wear bark and sleep in trees..."

"Don't be a chicken." She knew she was being childish.

"Don't be a scaredy-cat," he shot back.

She burst out laughing.

That night she stayed with him. But they did not cross that boundary to intimacy, even though every fibre in their being wanted to. Their guilt was stronger.

Before leaving, Heng embraced Yan, his arms warm around her shoulders. "Forget me. Start a new life."

"Take care of yourself." Yan tried to smile.

In the five years since their last meeting, she had tried to start a new life. She had gotten a job as an herbalist in a hospital. That's where she had met Han. He was persistent and so, a year later, she finally agreed to marry him, convinced that becoming a wife, and eventually a mother, would put an end to her memories of Heng.

***

She hesitated a second, but could not stop herself from writing down Heng's phone number. He was the only person she might want to talk to.

That night she dreamt that she was mired in a swamp, and overgrown shrubs and hedges were closing in on her. But many of the plants were medicinal herbs: Joe Pye weed, foxglove, lamb's ear, purple spike, pink-and-white twin lotuses, and marshmallow sprouted among the green bushes over which climbed a bright green Virginia snakeroot. A light blue mist floated above the distant wood like a veil.

To her surprise, Yan spied a giant striding past the marsh. He reached the wood in only two steps and then vanished. She tried to walk but could not take even one step in the long and clinging grass. With every move, she felt herself sink into the marsh. A multicoloured flower beckoned to her from a distance. When she finally managed to stagger toward the flower, the head of an alligator lunged at her unexpectedly. Frightened, she turned around, trying to escape. As she ran away from the alligator, she slammed into the giant's chest and her hands grabbed a button from his shirt. She opened her mouth to scream, but no sound came out.

After she woke, her arms still ached. She could not fall back asleep. Instead of tossing in bed, she decided to get up and turn on the light. She wrote about her dream in her diary: "I'm scared by this peculiar dream. I encountered a giant, a multicoloured flower, many other beautiful plants, and an alligator in a swampland. The twin lotuses are a symbol of love, but what do the other plants mean?"

She sighed and looked at her watch. It was midnight, the first time she could not sleep since leaving China. Wordless and melancholy, she doubted she could forget what she should have forgotten long ago.

She opened her notebook and found Heng's phone number. Her heart racing, she dialled the number. When she heard his voice, she whispered, "Heng," and then fell silent.

"Yan?" His voice was warm and calm.

"I – I –," she stuttered, not knowing where to begin, what to say.

"Where are you?" he asked, concerned.

"In New Orleans. Where are you?"

"I'm in Phoenix. How did you end up in New Orleans? You should contact your parents. You know, you've scared everyone."

"How did you know that I had left China?"

"My mother called me."

"Please don't tell anyone where I am. I needed to get away from Han."

"Why? You're being irrational. Your parents are extremely worried." Taking a breath, he asked, "Why didn't you call me earlier?"

"We should forget each other. You said that, didn't you? You've never dropped me a single line."

"I know." He was silent for a moment. "I'm working at a law firm. Why don't you come here? We can talk about this in person. I'll take a few days off."

"I'll come, but first promise me you won't tell anyone where I am. I'll explain when I see you."

Heng agreed. They talked a long time over the phone. Yan's heart felt suddenly full.

A week later, a Greyhound bus arrived in Phoenix. Yan got off the bus along with throngs of other passengers. Her eyes darted around the station as she searched for a familiar face among those waiting.

"Yan!"

Upon hearing his voice, Yan's heart skipped a beat. She turned her head and saw him. He had a white patch over his left eye. He was smiling at her. "Heng!" she called out, walking slowly toward him, suddenly not sure of herself or what she was doing. "What's wrong with your eye?" She asked when she finally reached him.

"I was stung by a wasp while driving yesterday. It'll be alright in a couple of days." As he spoke, he covered her hands with his.

"You're a one-eyed ogre!" she teased, thinking of her favourite childhood fairytale, the one they had read to each other over and over again.

He took her suitcase and teased back, "Sure, and you're like a puppy at my heels!"

Yan chuckled, pleased that he remembered the nickname he had given her so long ago. She said to Heng, "I can treat your wasp bite with lamb's ear." Laughing at Heng's confused expression, Yan explained, "It has nothing to do with a lamb. It's the name of an herb."

They walked out of the bus terminal, hand in hand. Yan was eager to talk to Heng about filing for a legal divorce by proxy in China, but she knew there was plenty of time for that. She also knew that in twenty-six states cousins are allowed to marry. *Did Heng know?* And as they walked further away from the bus station, she remembered the store-owner's wolfberry shrub and smiled. She would plant one, too.

A MANDARIN DUCK

"**M**OM, IS THIS OUR NEW HOME?" asked Wade who squatted to open a toy box near the window.

"Yeah. Do you like it?" Huidi was unpacking a suitcase in her son's bedroom.

"I guess it's okay, but I don't know any kids here," said Wade, pushing his toy car across the wooden floor.

"You'll make some new friends here."

"Can I go play outside?" The boy eased up, looking out the window. "I see some kids in the yard next door."

"Okay. Don't go far." Huidi started hanging up Wade's clothes in the closet. She pulled open the drawers, sorted underwear and socks, putting each in its respective place. Then, she pulled out a set of sheets, made the bed, and placed the toy box in a corner near her son's bed.

Huidi then made her way to her own bedroom to unpack her things and prepare her bed. She had mixed feelings about moving out of the transition house where they had lived for almost a year. She felt sad about leaving a place that had become "home," yet she was happy for her newly found independence. Too, she feared being out on her own. She wanted to make a good life for her son and decided to call her new home "independence." The full-time job she found in a cafeteria at the nearby university campus would make it possible for her to keep up with the rent.

When Huidi and her son sat at the kitchen table for supper later that evening, the room suddenly seemed empty and she found herself think-ing about her first day at the transition house sponsored by the Advisory Council on the Status of Women in Sackville, New Brunswick.

***

The kitchen was large and could easily seat ten people. The sunlight passed through its two windows, between which a huge table stood with a few chairs around it. A tall, blonde woman in her early forties was clearing the table. Huidi had met her earlier. The woman's name was on the tip of her tongue. Then she remembered. "Hi! Susan, is – are you busy?" Huidi tried to use the correct verb. She hadn't been in Canada long and her English was not very good. Until she left her husband, she hadn't had much occasion to practice.

"Not really. Do you need anything?" Susan raised her eyes, smiling.

"Yeah, something for lunch."

"You can have tuna sandwiches if you like." Susan opened the fridge and took out a plate of sandwiches. "I've made some for you."

"Thanks," said Huidi. "How much I own, no. I owe you?" She mo-tioned to Wade to come and sit at the table beside her.

"We only pay for things here once a month. I'll let you know at the end of the month," Susan replied, placing the plate of sandwiches on the table. "Help yourself. Plates and glasses are in the cupboard." She turned to Huidi's son and asked, "What's your name?"

"Wade." The boy looked at Susan, his eyes wide with curiosity. He had spotted a chest full of children's toys in the room beside the kitchen.

"Oh, that's a nice name. Wade, do you want milk or juice?"

"Juice, please." He was only five, but after two years in Canada, his English was much better than Huidi's.

Susan poured apple juice into a glass from a pitcher in the refrigerator and passed it to Wade, a wide, encouraging smile on her face. "After lunch, you can go play with the toys in the living room over there. "

"Thank you," said Wade very politely as he took the glass from her hand and placed it gingerly on the table in front of him.

"Susan, please what I can help do?" Huidi asked, picking up a sand-wich and handing it to her son beside her. "I like help here. "

"You know there are three mothers in the house including you. We share housekeeping duties. You'll meet Janice later. She has a boy, just one year old." Susan sat at the table and drank water from a glass. "Do you work?"

"I used to be kitchen help, but now I only care my son," said Huidi. "You?"

"A homemaker," Susan said, adding as an afterthought, "I'm separated."

"Why?"

"He was having an affair with another woman. I wouldn't stand for that and wanted a divorce, but he wouldn't agree," answered Susan, frowning. "Then he got very mean."

"I've divorced," Huidi sighed.

"Why?"

"My ex-husband beat Wade, then he beat me if I try to stop him. He not like Canada and he change here."

"Good for you to have left him," Susan smiled encouragingly.

"Without help from here, I would not know what do." Huidi's eyes looked perplexed. "My ex would hit Wade because he not want learn Chinese writing."

"Beating children, and women, is against the law." Susan raised her eyebrows.

"I thought father try give child lesson, but he beat too much Wade, too much." Huidi put her arm protectively around her son's shoulder. Noticing that the boy had eaten up his sandwich, she said, "You okay play now."

Susan said, "Wade, you can play with my daughter later too when she comes back from her drawing class."

"Okay." Wade smiled, hopping off his chair and heading for the toy chest.

A few days later, it was Huidi's turn to cook. That Saturday morning she had gone to the supermarket as soon as its doors had opened. Besides fish, meat, eggs, vegetables, and rice, she also picked up ginger, green onions, garlic, and soy sauce.

After she returned with the groceries, she got busy washing vegetables and cutting the fish and meat into bite-size pieces. She wanted to make a good lunch. Altogether, Huidi cooked four dishes: sweet and sour diced chicken with green peppers, salmon in tomato sauce, stir-fried pork with green beans and onions, and a bowl of mung bean sprout soup with shredded egg.

It was a happy lunch and everyone enjoyed the food. There were three mothers in the house and a number of children who played well together. At suppertime, Huidi stir-fried rice with the leftover food from lunch, and made tomato soup. After supper, Susan, in charge of the food budget, said, "Huidi, it'll cost too much money to keep eating like this."

"No, no," said Huidi, taking the receipt from the store out of her purse. "I calculate how much for two supper. Only $28. About $8 for adult and $2 for child."

"Really?" Susan couldn't believe it.

"I buy only what on special and cut up for cooking after get rid of unwanted parts."

"Gotcha!" Susan said. "You've got a head for this."

"You're smart," said Janice, "I bet it would be at least fifteen bucks a person if we ordered these dishes from any restaurant."

Huidi loved these meals, the camaraderie.

***

"Mom, when are you going to buy a TV set?" Wade's question brought Huidi back to the present.

"Soon," she said. "I'll check some flyers when I go to work on Monday." She cleared the table. "You should do your homework now."

Wade was Huidi's main focus. She hoped her son would go to university to make up for what she had missed. She even paid a tutor to teach Wade French on weekends. There was little for her to do in the small town they were living in, and she hadn't been able to make any new friends with whom she could share her loneliness, her worries, her dreams. Meeting Chinese people was difficult as there wasn't even a Chinese grocery store in town. Once she called a Chinese woman she had known before leaving her husband, but the woman never phoned back. Maybe she thought that Huidi was insane for not hiding her family problems and for divorcing her husband. A male co-worker had once asked her out on a date, but she declined. Even though she had been familiar with faces that were different from Chinese faces, she could not yet understand what was behind blue or hazel eyes. She missed Shanghai very much. A few times, she dreamt that she was lost on her favourite bustling street in Shanghai, unable to find her way home and woke up wondering why she was living in a strange country.

Her only contact was Sandy from the Advisory Council that was in charge of the transition house. From Sandy she heard cheerful news about Susan, who had at last divorced her husband and was happily studying in the Social Work programme at Mount Allison University, and Janice, who was in a six-month training programme and planned on starting up day-care services in her home following her graduation. Huidi felt happy for them but sad for herself. When she lived in the transition house, like Susan and Janice, she had participated in some meetings arranged by the Council and learned about how important it was for women to have life skills. She had begun to understand a link between education and economic independence. So Huidi decided to go to university, and registered for a Home Economics course at Mount Allison.

That September, Huidi and her son left for school in the early morning and returned in the late afternoon. Out of school for sixteen years and with a limited English vocabulary, Huidi found it hard to be a student. The methods of teaching and learning were so different from what she was used to in China. Once, her mind went blank when the students had a group discussion about how consumer choice affected the market. When it was her turn, she couldn't think of anything to say.

She had encountered some Chinese students on campus, and wondered if they could help her with her English, and her loneliness. But they were busy with their studies and saying "Hi" in passing seemed to be her only connection to them.

After several weeks of struggle, she narrowly passed only one of three quizzes and had to withdraw from the course. Her bubble burst. And she realized that her limited knowledge of the English language was isolating her in more ways than one.

***

One morning, Huidi served breakfast at the cafeteria's front counter.

Her job was to fill the plates with bacon and eggs, or pancakes and sausages, or muffin and fruit, and pass them over the counter.

"Next!" She was passing another filled plate to the next person in line, when she heard a man's voice call out, "Pancakes and sausages, please!"

She recognized the familiar foreign accent in his English. Raising her eyes, she saw the broad face of a Chinese man who looked to be in his middle forties. His eyes were bloodshot under his glasses.

"Wait a moment," answered Huidi, striding to the kitchen. In a few moments, she was back with a plate of freshly cooked pancakes. When she passed the plate to the man, she could not help but ask, "You from mainland China?"

"Yes. You, too?" replied the broad-faced man as he took his plate.

"Yes," she said in Chinese, her eyes flashing. "How about you? What are you doing here?"

"I am doing research."

"That's interesting. The milk and sugar for coffee are just over there," she said, pointing to a stand next to the counter.

"Thanks," answered the man. He went to the cashier and then found a table to eat his breakfast.

***

A week went by. Friday afternoon came again. There were many bright orange jack-o'-lanterns on display near the front steps of many houses as she made her way home. Numerous ghost masks and skulls covered with black or white veils hung from tree branches. A few dangling porch skeletons, spookily lit up, swayed slightly in the wind.

Ugh, Halloween again, she thought. She did not like this festival. To her, ghost masks and dangling skeletons were ominous signs of death and bad luck.

At supper, Wade could hardly sit still. "Mamma, remember? Tonight I'm going to meet my classmate, Yolande," his voice filled with excitement. "We're going for 'trick or treat.'" Huidi had reluctantly agreed to let Wade take part in this strange festival. She wanted him to fit in, have friends. Wade wolfed through his supper and as soon as Huidi had also finished, he pulled on the bullhead mask she had finally agreed to

120

buy him and dragged his mother out of the apartment building. They walked to the corner to wait for Wade's friend and watched the clusters of children dressed as witches, monsters, and ghosts clattering down the street. It wasn't long before they spied a little girl wearing a green dress and a headband with a fringe of sunflower petals, skipping down the street toward them, her mother in tow.

"Yolande!"

"Wade!" The two children cheerfully joined hands and bounced down the street together, leaving the two mothers behind.

The children knocked on the doors of every house on one side of the street. They were thrilled with each offering of treats. When their bags were almost full, Wade and Yolande plunked down on the sidewalk and counted their candy and apples: "Two! Four! Six…" they shouted gleefully in unison.

Yolande looked up and saw her mother coming toward her. "Leave me alone, Mommy!" She stamped her feet. "Don't come here!"

"Help me with my bag, Mamma!" Wade asked his mother. Suddenly he realized he was not supposed to let his mother take him home, so he waved his hand. "Mamma, don't come."

The two children happily resumed trick-or-treating on the other side of the street, and their mothers continued to follow them. Although Huidi found it difficult at first to talk to Yolande's mother, gradually the two women turned from strangers into walking partners, sharing small pieces of their lives. When it got late, the children dragged their feet. Waving goodbye to each other, the women hurriedly took their children back home, one hand holding the child's hand, the other a sack of candy.

Wade pulled away from Huidi to run joyfully ahead of her. Suddenly, he tripped, landing face-first on the sidewalk. He burst into tears, "Mamma, Mamma!" Huidi bent over him and immediately saw a big gash on his forehead. It was bleeding profusely. "Hold on, Wade. I think we need to go to the hospital." She carefully pulled her son onto her back and shakily stood up under the streetlight.

"Do you need help?" A Chinese voice with a Suzhou accent came from a figure in front of her.

Huidi saw the broad-faced man that she had met when serving

breakfast earlier that week. Glad and surprised, she answered, "Yes, please. We must go to the emergency room." It was a relief to be able to speak Chinese.

The man easily shifted Wade from her back to his. "Where is the hospital?"

"Not far from here." Huidi hurried with the candy sack, leading the way toward the hospital that thankfully was nearby.

"Do you enjoy Halloween?" asked the man.

"Not at all. I should have known I would have bad luck." Huidi sighed.

"What bad luck?" asked the man.

"You can see for yourself. My son hurt himself."

"I know you're probably uncomfortable with these strange decorations. I was too. It is indeed an odd custom."

Huidi felt as though he had looked right through her. She wondered if he had also taken a youngster out that night.

The man seemed to be able to read her mind. "I was on my way home from the library."

Wade sat glumly on the examination table, his eyes wincing as the doctor closed the gash on his forehead with three stitches and then bandaged the wound. "I wanna go home, Mamma."

The man had stayed with them throughout the procedure. His name was Peng. While they were waiting to be seen, he told Huidi he was a lecturer at a university in Beijing and had come to Canada to do research on the administration of Canadian universities. He had come to New Brunswick after half a year in Toronto with two other Chinese researchers who were doing similar work. Huidi wondered why he would choose to come to a place like Sackville. "I selected Mount Allison University for my case study because of its long history. It has a reputation for opening the first girls' college and recruiting the first few female students in a university degree programme in Canada," he said, as they waited for the doctor to finish.

"I'll take you home now," Peng said as he carried the boy out of the hospital. A smile on Huidi's face showed her appreciation. By the time they reached Huidi's apartment it was almost 11 p.m. Exhausted, Wade fell asleep as soon as Huidi put him to bed.

"Please stay for some tea," Huidi said. She filled a plate with cookies and put a kettle of water on the stove. She wanted to know more about him.

"Did you know that in 1875, Grace Annie Lockhart graduated from Mount Allison and became the first woman to receive a bachelor's degree in the British Empire?" Peng said, accepting the cup of tea Huidi placed in front of him at the kitchen table.

She was not interested in his topic. History had nothing to do with her. What she faced was an uncertain future. "How long will you stay here?"

"If I can get an additional grant, I'd stay for another half a year."

"I miss Shanghai a lot." It was not often Huidi had a chance to speak Chinese, so she was eager to talk about her life.

"If it's too difficult for you here, you could go back."

"When I think about my son's future I know I have to stay." As she said this, Huidi felt tears well up in her eyes. Huidi told him how hard it had been after leaving her abusive husband to start a new life, how lonely she was in Sackville, and how hard she was finding it to make friends.

The tea finished, and the cookies eaten, it was time for Peng to leave. Huidi saw him to the door. Turning his head, Peng was touched by the sad and lonely expression on her face. Suddenly, passionately, he pulled her into his arms. *I don't need to sleep in an empty bed tonight*, he thought. To his surprise, Huidi did not resist, but leaned her head on his chest.

That night, he lost sight of his wife, and she forgot her days without a man.

The next morning, she got up early as usual. She helped Wade dress and served him his breakfast. Wade found Peng in his mother's bedroom and clapped his hands. "Mamma's boyfriend is a lazy-bones!"

When Peng woke up, Wade was playing outside. He felt at home. He enjoyed the breakfast that Huidi had prepared for him and she felt happy watching him eat. She was only mildly disappointed when he told her he had a wife and a child in China.

A few days later, he moved in and told Huidi he would pay her $300 for a month's rent plus breakfast and supper. Considering he might be short of money, she only accepted $250.

Peng had a travel bag that looked suspiciously large. Inside were piles of made-in-China instant noodle packages. With her help, he put away his food supply.

"I've been eating bags of noodles like this to save money. It's made me lose my appetite," he chuckled.

"From now on, you don't need to eat these noodles. You can eat my food." She smiled at him.

"I'm looking forward to that," he said. "I'll take what's left of these to the university for lunch."

***

The days went by smoothly and quickly. Huidi had a man; Wade had a father figure; and Peng had home-cooked meals and a warm body next to him at night.

One Saturday afternoon, Huidi decided to prepare a few fancy dishes for a special meal. Peng offered to help and rinsed the vegetables while she basted the duck they had managed to find in the supermarket for roasting. "Would you like to live in Canada?" she asked while setting a pot on a burner. She wasn't sure how to turn the conversation to what mattered most to her.

"You mean to live here for good?" He gave a wry smile. "What kind of job could I get?"

"Work at the university?" Huidi placed another pan on the stove.

"You're kidding," he said with a smirk. "It would take me at least five years to get a Ph.D. Even then I might not find a teaching position."

"You could open a convenience store and that will make enough money," she said as she began stir-frying the vegetables.

"A store? That isn't the type of work I want to do. Besides, I'll be promoted to an associate professor when I go back to Beijing." He cleaned up the counter while Huidi heaped steamed rice into a serving bowl.

"All jobs are the same to me as long as they bring in enough income."

"Remember? I have a wife and a daughter. It's hard for me to make a decision about staying in Canada."

"What does your wife do?" She felt curious.

"Let's change the topic." He sat down as Huidi placed the steamed rice and a platter of stir-fried vegetables on the table.

"Why do you live with me?" she muttered as she sat down across from him. She had wanted this evening to be special. The conversation wasn't going in the direction she had hoped for.

"What?" he asked. He was looking at her curiously and sniffing. "Something's burning."

"That's my duck!" she yelled as she jumped up and then pulled open the oven door. She should have turned the oven down an hour ago. The stench of burnt meat spread throughout the kitchen.

"We talked too much and forgot what we were doing." Peng said, moving to the window to let in some fresh air.

Huidi dumped the charred dish and scraped the pan. *What does he think about living with me?* she wondered, not able to shake off the feeling that the burnt duck might be an omen. She remembered that the mandarin duck was a traditional Chinese symbol for lovers. *Why*, Huidi thought, *can't we live together like mandarin ducks?*

***

That evening, they all watched television until Huidi persuaded her son to go to bed. When she returned, she sat on the couch next to Peng. With a deep breath, she asked, "Why do you live with me?"

"I don't know." He turned his head. "Because you're nice."

"But you have a wife." She raised her voice.

"You don't want me? I can move out if you don't want me," he chuckled. "Is that what you want?" His eyes seemed to mock her.

"No, I mean…" She searched her mind for the right word.

"You mean I shouldn't be living with you?"

"No, I mean you should think about living with me." She stared into his face.

"Now I am living with you. What else do you want?"

"You know what I mean."

"I don't even know myself," he said, shaking his head. "If you want me to go, I will. If you want me to stay, don't ask too much."

"Sorry," said Huidi. She didn't want him to leave. But she didn't know how to convince him to stay with her permanently. "I hope you will stay."

"Let's just see what happens." He reached for her hands. "Cheer up. There's no point talking about the unknown."

***

Christmas was around the corner. Huidi bought some indoor Christmas lights and hung them along the window frame.

"What's bothering you?" she asked as she glanced at Peng's troubled face.

"This year is almost over," he sighed.

"Don't you like Christmas?"

He did not answer, so she stopped asking.

A few days later, Huidi arrived home from work with a look of excitement on her face. "Peng!" She took out an invitation card from her manager and said, "Look! We're gonna have a Christmas party this coming Friday. I want you to go with me. Can you come?"

"Oh, no. I have some odds and ends to take care of." He shrugged.

"Come on. I won't go if you don't go," she said, trying to hide the disappointment in her voice. She hoped he would change his mind.

"This coming Friday?" He looked at the calendar and shook his head. "I can't find the time for it. But it will be fun and you and Wade must go."

At five o'clock on Friday afternoon, Huidi and Wade went to the Christmas party at the cafeteria. There was lots of relaxed and happy chatter. Dishes with all kinds of different foods were laid out on several tables. Platters of sweets turned Wade's eyes into saucers. But Huidi could not enjoy it. It was past ten o'clock when she got home only to find that Peng was not there. *Maybe he is still working on his report in the computer lab*, she thought.

Her heart sank the next morning when she opened her eyes and touched the empty pillow beside her. She turned over and got up to pull open the closet doors. His clothes and suitcases were gone. Unable to hold herself up, she fell to the floor and wept. She knew he had left her life. And now she was alone again.

***

Time flew.

When Huidi received the December phone bill, she stared at the figure on the paper. The long distance charges came to $443.69, but Peng had evaporated like a dream. Damn! She had to pay the bill by using some of the money she had saved for emergencies.

Day by day, week by week, she gradually began to feel better. In February, she received a letter without a return address on the envelope. She tore it open.

Feb. 1, 1996
Huidi,

Sorry for leaving you without saying goodbye. I can't explain why. I'm enclosing a cheque of $200 for the long distance calls I made before I left. If the money is not enough for the bill, consider the difference as my fee for tutoring Wade.

Best wishes for the Chinese Year of the Rat!
Peng

Huidi turned the letter over but could not find his name nor a mailing address on the envelope. She only identified a few Chinese characters: Beijing, China.

She sighed and threw the envelope into a trash basket.

Sitting at the table, she was lost in thought: *Speaking Chinese is easier. But then I might only meet people like Peng. And just like him, others might try and take advantage of me. He never even told me his full name. Now two men in my life have abused me. Never again. I must learn to speak English. I know I can learn.* Finally she picked up the phone and dialled Sandy's number. She regretted she hadn't called her more often.

"It's Huidi calling." She was eager to talk when she heard Sandy's voice. "Can you help me find some information about ESL classes?"

"I sure can," answered Sandy in a surprised voice. "Are you sure you can spare the time? I know you are working full-time."

"Yeah, important to improve English. I am ready to sign up for ESL class."

"Great. I'm sure you can make some friends in that class, too," added Sandy.

"Do you think they have evening classes?"

"Evening classes? Maybe. I can ask about childcare for ESL learners, too. When can you start?"

"Right now!" Huidi felt better after speaking with Sandy, happy with her decision. She could live in Canada not only for her son, but also for herself.

NOODLES

FANNY STRUGGLED TO EAT NOODLES out of a bowl filled with shrimp-flavoured soup using her fork.

"Why don't you just use chopsticks instead?" asked her husband, Ah Ming, who was putting on his backpack, amused by Fanny's attempts to spear the noodles with her fork. He did not wait for her answer. "I'm leaving. Are you sure you don't need me to go with you?"

"It's only two blocks away. I can find it by myself." Fanny continued working on her noodles. Fanny, from a small town in China, had joined Ah Ming in Toronto only a few weeks before. Everything had interested her. However, she was frustrated by the fact that she could not understand English despite having taken lessons before coming. Everyone spoke so fast. Although Ah Ming told her to take it easy, and not to worry about it too much, Fanny had already signed up for a free English as a Second Language course for newcomers sponsored by the United Church in the neighbourhood.

Finally she swallowed the last sip of the noodle soup. She felt triumphant at not having had to resort to chopsticks. With a book bag on her shoulder, she left home. Walking past the pedestrians in the morning rush hour, she felt as if she had become a schoolgirl again, hurrying to her classes. Her goal was not to be late. She walked quickly until she finally reached the Church. Following the sign pointing to the ESL classroom in the basement, she was happy to find a roomy space. The door was wide open, and other students were arriving. Colourful pictures of the English alphabet hung on the walls around the classroom. Fanny chose a desk in the back of the room that would give her a good view of the teacher who had short blonde hair and was wearing a pink blouse and black skirt. There were about fifteen students in the class. She had a welcoming smile for all of them.

"Good morning. Welcome to class." The woman instructor's voice was smooth and pleasant, but Fanny did not know how to respond to her greeting. She could only smile.

"My name is Gay MacDonald," said the instructor. "I'm a student in the Ph.D. program in the Linguistics Department at the University of Toronto, and a volunteer teacher in the adult ESL program."

Then she asked all the students to talk a little about themselves.

"Hi. I'm Usha from India. Nice to meet all of you."

"I'm from Albania."

"I'm José and I'm from Cuba."

"I'm from Pakistan."

Fanny discovered the world was small after she heard a voice from behind her say, "I'm from China."

Fanny turned her head toward the young woman who had spoken. Delighted to meet a classmate from her country of origin, she asked her, "Which province are you from?"

"Guangdong. And you?" answered the young woman who reached out her hand in greeting.

"Me, too." Fanny grasped her classmate's hand.

Fanny's eyes misted. Meeting people from her home country always warmed her heart. It reminded her of another encounter a couple of days earlier.

At a local grocery store, Fanny had pushed a buggy down an aisle, her eyes scanning the shelves lined with colourful cans, boxes, and containers. Her buggy had run into a woman who was reading the label on a box of cake mix. The woman looked Chinese. The moment had offered Fanny her first chance to speak to someone from her home country, so she had greeted the woman in Chinese, "*Ni-hao!* Are you from China?"

"Err…" The woman had looked blankly at Fanny. "Are you from the U of T?"

"No," Fanny had replied in Chinese, "but my husband is a student at the university. How long have you been here? Do you know…?"

"I've been here for a long time," the woman had answered in English. She looked older than Fanny and smiled only a little. She seemed to understand Fanny but would not speak in Chinese. "Excuse me." The woman did not show any interest in the conversation and said, "I've got to run."

Before Fanny had a chance to say goodbye, the woman had vanished down the aisle. *Why is she so unsociable, just like a "foreigner?"* In her mind, "foreigners" always kept their distance from one another. Fanny used to call non-Chinese people "foreigners" in China and even now, in Canada, she still thought of non-Chinese people as "foreigners." But this woman was obviously from here, maybe even born here. And Fanny suddenly realized that she was the "foreigner" now.

The instructor's voice dragged Fanny back to the present. "Let me tell you something about my teaching plan first; and then you can tell me your expectations for this course."

Fanny could only catch a few sentences. She wondered if the others could understand everything the instructor said. A young fellow next to her appeared to enjoy the lecture immensely. He had light brown skin and curly hair. The man listened with smiles and asked questions in a clear voice. A sour feeling swelled over Fanny as she thought about taking English courses in China. As a university student, she had found the English course the hardest nut to crack. She could memorize a large vocabulary, but always had trouble with pronunciation and intonation. She was uncertain if there was something wrong with the teacher's pronunciation or if her ears had a problem. Since then, her hair had stood on end whenever she heard anyone speak English.

But, something was different in this class. Fanny found herself less nervous when listening to the instructor, who combined body language and situational conversation in English. And Fanny's vocal muscles felt less tense when she practiced daily conversation with other students, many of whom were struggling as hard as she was to learn. However, English words still sounded like gusts of wind that came in one ear and went out the other. She had trouble keeping them in. Midway through the class, her head seemed to have turned into a big bowl full of paste.

Later, the paste became dough that got sliced into long noodles that hung there, one by one, waiting for her to use them for something.

While working on a writing assignment at home, she got confused trying to use those English "noodles." She was unable to distinguish one noodle from the other. She decided to ask Ms. MacDonald for help. After carefully planning what she would say on the phone, Fanny dialled her teacher's number.

"Hello, may I speak to Gay?" She still winced whenever she called her instructor by her first name. In China, that would be seen as disrespectful. *When in Rome, do as the Romans do.* Fanny wanted so much to fit in.

A hoarse voice came through the phone line. "Speaking."

It was a woman's voice, but it was so hoarse that it took Fanny aback. *Is this Gay? Is she sick?* Fanny was confused. "Are you Gay?" she asked hesitantly, embarrassed to think she might be disturbing her instructor on a day she was not well.

"No, no. It's…"

Puzzled, Fanny hastily hung up. At that moment, all her English "noodles" collapsed into a big ball of gooey dough. Now she was not sure whom she had dialled. Later she learned that "gay" was a word for homosexuals. She realized she should have asked, "Is this Gay?" instead of "Are you Gay?" She worried about whom she may have offended with her mixed-up English.

Several weeks later, Fanny took a trip with her class to G. Ross Lord Park. They walked through a meadow with many trees. Purple, pink, and butter-yellow wild flowers blanketed the meadow and swayed easily with the breeze. Birds chirped in almost every tree they passed. The park was quiet and so different from the parks she had visited in China. In China, the parks were gated, and were no more than cultivated gardens surrounded by fences, criss-crossed with concrete paths and filled with crowded pavilions. For Fanny, the park they were visiting was like a big open field in the wild.

While enjoying the fresh air and taking in the views of the field, Fanny snacked on a box of raisins. When she was finished, she tossed the empty box onto the grass. She was surprised to glimpse a Canadian man picking up the tiny carton she had thrown and slip it into his pocket.

Knowing that some people collected pictures on matchboxes, Fanny thought, *People in Canada must collect pictures on all kinds of boxes.*

At lunchtime, some of her classmates put several picnic tables together and everybody placed his or her potluck offering on the large wood surface. Fanny recognized the young man who had picked up her empty raisin box. She watched him when he strode purposely toward the trash can and fished something out of his pocket. When Fanny realized he was tossing her raisin box into the trash, her face flushed crimson.

"Does anybody like pizza?" Gay pointed to a large, flat box on the table, smiling. "Please help yourselves." The pepperoni, red tomato, green pepper, and mushrooms that topped the pizza looked so inviting. Fanny helped herself to a slice. It was her first taste of pizza.

"Oh, it's very delicious," one student said after he bit noisily into a slice. "Did you make it yourself?" he asked Gay.

"No, but my boyfriend Larry did," replied Gay, a tone of pride in her voice, her hand gesturing to the young man who had thrown Fanny's box into the trashcan. "He works at Pizza Hut."

A number of students began clapping their hands.

How could a Ph.D. student fall in love with a cook? Fanny thought with astonishment. According to the Chinese way, the man should always be in a higher position than his woman. This pair was the opposite.

Fanny was bewildered by many things that day. She wondered if she was experiencing "culture shock"—she had learned the phrase from her instructor. It was as if her cooked English "noodles" had been smothered in cranberry sauce with chilli, a confusing and odd combination.

***

A year later, after his graduation, Fanny's husband, Ah Ming, found a job. Fanny had made good progress in English. She spoke English to anyone except her husband, and, she could use a fork to eat any kind of food except soup.

The couple's favourite meal was Fanny's noodles with sweet and sour pork chops. First, she fried the chops in a bit of oil until they turned golden yellow, then she poured the sweet and sour sauce mixed with finely chopped ginger, onion, and garlic over top. Simmering the meat for a few minutes was the last step in the cooking process. The noodles, prepared separately, made a bed for the pork chops and their sauce. This dish was so delicious that they both felt it could easily compete with the famous full-course meals made especially for high-ranking officials in the Qing Dynasty.

One evening, after a meal of Fanny's special noodles, Ah Ming slouched on the couch contentedly and watched television. Fanny passed a cup of tea to him and peeled an orange for herself. Then she sat down to enjoy the TV too. On the screen, a chubby baby boy, perched on a huge tire, floated down from the sky. The boy's wide-open, toothless smile teased Ah Ming. *I'm already in my thirties and should be a dad by now.* As he thought about this, he glanced at Fanny. She looked hesitant, and then said, "I have something to tell you."

"What is it? I'm listening." Noticing the serious expression on Fanny's face, Ah Ming was amused. "Now, don't look so serious," he teased. "I just want to know if you want to have a baby?"

"No, no!" Fanny shook her head vigorously from side to side. "I mean, I may... I may ..."

"What?" Ah Ming exclaimed. "You're pregnant?" His eyes were wide with surprise. He placed his cup down on the coffee table and turned to Fanny. He took both of her hands in his. "This is great! Just great!" *God, my wish is coming true,* he thought.

"I am not a hundred percent sure yet, Ah Ming," Fanny said, pulling her hands away. "And I really would prefer to put it off. I want to get my Master's degree before having a baby."

"What?" Ah Ming's lips trembled. "Having a kid at an older age is not good for a mother or her baby," he said.

"I'm not even thirty. Many women in this country have their first babies after thirty-five. Age doesn't matter." She poured out her ideas like water running out of a faucet that had just turned on. "If I hold a degree from a Canadian university, I can find a decent job. Then we don't need to worry about money should you get laid off."

Ah Ming was shocked. "Just hold on," he said. "We are Chinese and you know men and women have very different roles. I'm the breadwinner and you look after our kids. That's just the way it is. You don't need a Master's degree to do that."

"Isn't it better if we both make a living and bring up our kids together?"

Fanny said, biting her lip anxiously. "We are in Canada now and people do things in a different way here."

Ah Ming's head began to throb. He did not understand why Fanny was acting this way. She had always been so accommodating. He looked at her curiously, wondering if he really knew her. "I don't know. I just don't know. Let me think it over," he said, in a voice that was not convincing even to himself.

"Still, I need to see a doctor and find out for certain one way or the other if I'm pregnant."

Ah Ming suddenly felt queasy. The food in his stomach was making him nauseous. Sweat appeared on his forehead as he pressed his hands on his stomach. "Fanny, I don't feel so good," he grumbled.

"Should I take you to the after-hours clinic?" asked Fanny as she wiped his forehead with some tissue.

"I think so." But Ah Ming's voice was feeble.

She turned off the television and grabbed the car keys on the table. Then Fanny held his arm and led him out the door.

Once outside, she noticed the streetlights already on, penetrating the endless, dark sky. She suddenly felt homesick. She remembered a voice in Cantonese: "A bowl of noodle soup. Always good. Always warm." It was the voice of the waitress that used to serve her in the small noodle restaurant Fanny frequented often in her hometown.

As they hurried to the clinic, Fanny wondered what she might have done differently this time to the noodles that had made her husband so violently ill. It was a dish she had made many times. One she had learned to eat successfully with a fork, despite Ah Ming's continued protests and insistence on using chopsticks. Maybe this time she had added too much chilli in the sauce. When they entered the clinic, Fanny helped Ah Ming to a chair and then realized that she had to find the washroom immediately. When she sat on the toilet, she thought she detected a drop of blood on her panties. She got up and splashed some cold water on her face, studying her features in the mirror carefully. She knew then that she wasn't pregnant. And she was relieved.

Anxious to know what had caused Ah Ming's stomach pain, she hurried over to her husband in the waiting room. He, too, had made his way to the bathroom where his stomach had heaved, his dinner expunged. But his face was still pale and his hands were clammy. When the doctor finally saw Ah Ming, he sent him home with a note for some over-the-counter medication for indigestion. "What do you think happened?" he asked Fanny, leaning slightly against her as they walked to the door.

Fanny smiled at him reassuringly. "I must have put too much chilli in the sauce. Don't worry, everything is okay."

GINKGO

ONE HOT, STICKY EVENING IN Shanghai, China, Rain wandered onto Huaihai Road in search of the cool breezes coming from the Huangpu River. The sidewalks were crowded with people waving paper or feather fans. Among the crowd was a pretty girl in her thirties, her long braids swinging behind her, her steps tapping to the music that flowed out from the open shops. She was coming toward him. Rain recognized her as the zither player he had met at her own farewell party a few days earlier. His friend, Zheng, was her cousin, and he had asked Rain to play clarinet at the party. Delighted, Rain walked toward her and asked, "Brook, how're you doing?"

"I'm doing fine." Her eyes shone when she saw him. "I remember you!" she exclaimed. "You played the clarinet exquisitely the night of my party."

"Your zither performance opened my eyes." Rain smiled and pointed to a nearby teahouse. "How about a cold drink?"

"Why not?"

She followed him into the Red Bean Teahouse and sat down at a table by the window. She asked for some gingko nut soup and he ordered a glass of iced tea.

"I'm leaving next week and feeling a little bit reluctant," she confessed. "I'll be living in a place that is strange and foreign to me, even if New York is a famous, and exciting, city."

"Have you met your future husband before?" asked Rain, boldly. At the party he had heard about her upcoming marriage to a prospective businessman.

"Yes … fifteen years ago, when he visited his relatives. They lived next door to my family," she answered in a flat voice as if she were telling another person's story. "But, I only agreed to marry him very recently."

"I heard about Den from your cousin. He told me about your engagement," he said, realizing that he had been staring at her face, unable to avert his gaze. Zheng had also told him about another man who had been in Brook's life when she was much younger. Zheng said she had been deeply in love with this man. "I'm wondering," he hesitated for a moment. "If things were different and you could change things that happened in the past, would you still marry Den in the States?"

"A missed chance won't come again," she lowered her voice. "I know my fate."

At that moment, they could not find anything else to say. Rain sipped his tea. Brook carefully spooned the ginkgo nut soup into her mouth. They were at a loss for words, but the electricity between them spoke enough. Rain recalled her farewell party.

Brook, in a white blouse and tight, red satin skirt, had sat on a chair, playing her Chinese zither with tiny, meticulous movements. Her braids were draped over her chest, two bright red hair bows on their ends. As her arms swayed, and her fingers played the strings quickly yet tenderly, the red bows fluttered like butterflies dancing on her chest. A composite of classical Chinese music, "Water Spirit in Hunan" flowed from her fingers like a creek tumbling through a quiet valley. After her performance, Rain had played a cheerful and humorous selection from "Le Nozze di Figaro" on his clarinet. He had noticed that Brook listened to his performance with joyous attention, her eyes betraying her enthusiasm for the melody. Touched, he had performed his best.

"Rain, I didn't expect your clarinet to blend so well with my Chinese music, 'Water Spirit in Hunan.'" Her voice dragged him back to the teahouse.

"I was surprised, too," he said, tapping his finger on the table cheerfully. "Chinese instruments never attracted me before, but your zither did."

"When did you start playing the clarinet?" she asked.

"In high school. I learned from my elder brother who'd played the oboe in a song and dance troupe."

"Ah, that's why you have an ear for music. I inherited mine from my father, who enjoyed playing the Chinese two-string violin. He trained me with the instrument when I was little, but my mother kept insisting that the two-string violin was not suitable for a girl. So I switched to the zither."

"Are you going to play it in the States?"

"Why not? I'll take my zither with me and practice it whenever I have time."

"Too bad I won't be able to hear you play again." He wanted to tell her how much he wished to hear her play again. Instead, he told her about having completed his degree and subsequently securing a job with the foreign trade department.

"Whoa! You should be carefree." Brook chuckled. "You're young and have a promising future." Thoughtfully, she added, "I returned to the city after a couple of years of re-education, forced upon us by Mao during the Cultural Revolution, and I could not even find a low-paying job." Brook's voice was calm, but her tone had a trace of downheartedness.

Rain placed his glass back on the table, and his fingers tapped it as if he were revealing his thoughts: *She's leaving and I won't see her anymore.*

They stared into each other's eyes, but said nothing. Again, a moment of silence wrapped them. When they left the Red Bean Teahouse, Rain remarked that in a popular ancient poem by Wang Wei of the Tang Dynasty, red beans are described as love seeds. They locked eyes, and shook each other's hand before turning in the opposite direction and walking away. Both were surprised when they caught themselves casting a glance back.

***

Eight years later, in New York City, the day before the Chinese New Year, clientele filled the Dragon Eyes Restaurant on Elizabeth Street. Among the patrons was a young couple having their lunch. They sat at a table behind screens painted with dancing dragons and phoenixes. Above them, on the wall, dim, pink light highlighted a picture of lotus flowers.

"Rain, take some of mine," said the woman, her hand delicately holding a glass of beer.

"Just leave it if you don't want it," answered Rain, staring at Plum's pink cheeks. He could not help but touch her face with his hand, a face that shone under the light. He smiled and leaned toward her. "Are you coming to my place tonight?"

"Yes." She rounded her lips, and asked, "When are you going to tell your parents about our relationship, you dutiful son?"

"It's too early yet. We're still young." In his early thirties, Rain still had plenty of time ahead of him. Why should he rush into a relationship?

"I'm already yours." Plum twisted her mouth into a wry smile. She was in her late twenties and was anxious to get married and start a family. "Do you mean you're dragging your feet only because we're young?"

"Hey, aren't you a modern girl?" Rain grinned at her, taking his hand away from her face. "God knows whether you'll meet a better man in the future. Enjoy your life now, and don't think about tomorrow."

Flipping her long hair over her shoulders, Plum glared at him. "I get it. Thanks a lot," she snipped.

"Okay, okay." Rain did not want upset her. He picked up a piece of bamboo shoot from a dish with his chopsticks and raised it to her mouth. "Come on now, gorgeous. Eat."

Rain's flattery made Plum happy, and his teasing made her snicker. "Nonsense talker," she said, flicking his forehead with her fingers.

After dinner, as they walked toward the entrance, Rain heard a man call, "Brook, did you forget your scarf?"

Brook? Rain turned his head and faced a woman in her late thirties standing just a few steps away. Her smiling eyes looked as if they were speaking. It was her! He could not believe his eyes. Time seemed to rewind; it was eight years earlier, and they were back in the Red Bean Teahouse on Huaihai Road. He could feel the heat from that street in Shanghai. Like a stream, eight years had passed through high mountains, low valleys, and joined the sea. He was seeing her again on this snow-covered day in another city far away. He greeted her with undisguised pleasure, "Brook! Hello!"

"Rain! What are you doing here? It is so nice to see you," she said, surprised and also pleased to see him.

Rain noticed that she held a child in each of her hands and asked,

"Are these your children?"

"Yes, they are!" Brook replied. "It's been so many years! How are you? When did you arrive in New York?"

"I got a job and moved here last year. The world is unbelievably small."

"What a coincidence!" She nodded and raised her chin to the man who had called to her earlier. "This is Den, my husband. Is this your wife?" She looked at the girl beside Rain.

"My girlfriend," he answered and then introduced her to Plum. "Brook is an old friend from China."

Rain stretched out his hand to Den, "I'm honoured to meet you." Noticing Den's puzzled eyes, he added, "Brook's cousin, Zheng, is my friend. He often talked about you."

"Ahh, I see ... Good to meet you," Den said, his eyebrows raised. "Please, join us for tea at our home." Den was very cordial.

"Our place is near here, only a few blocks away," Brook added.

Rain rubbed his hands with excitement. "Sure. We'd love to."

Brook's face lit up. "Let's go."

***

Rain's car followed Den's down Elizabeth Street and onto Spring Street, stopping in front of a bungalow guarded by two stone lions.

Rain and Plum followed the family into the house. Den was carrying his young son who had fallen asleep in the car. Den continued on toward his son's bedroom, while Brook guided the guests into the living room. "Please have a seat," she said. Her voice was warm and inviting.

She placed some toys in front of her daughter, after plopping her down in a corner of the living room. "I'll be right back," she said as she turned toward the kitchen.

Den came back to the living room, and took a seat next to Rain. "Are you engaged?" he asked, smiling pointedly first at Rain, then at Plum.

"Not yet." Rain said, his eyes meeting Plum's expectant ones for just a moment.

Den noticed. "Don't miss out on your chance, lucky guy."

"He can wait because he's still young," Plum said, the bitterness in her voice unconcealed.

"Den, you have a nice house and family," Rain said, trying to shift the focus from his relationship with Plum. "You must've worked hard for years."

"Right," Den said, "and it wasn't easy."

Brook returned from the kitchen and placed a teapot and cups on the coffee table along with a tray of cookies and candy. "Please help yourselves," she said, gesturing to the platter. When they had finished their tea, Den offered to show Plum around the house. Rain and Brook remained chatting in the living room.

"How have you been all these years?" Rain asked. "Has your life here been good?"

"It's good." She smiled. "What about you? It's a real surprise seeing you again," she said, her pulse quickening.

"The years have passed like a fast-moving stream." Rain shook his head ruefully, his eyes locked on hers. "I regret…"

"Youth is priceless," Brook interrupted. "Even gold can't buy it back. You're both young, and Plum is beautiful. I think she really loves you."

"Do you still play the zither?" Rain changed the topic.

"I've only played twice since I came here. I don't have an audience, you know. Do you still play the clarinet?"

"I haven't played it for ages. I've been too busy either studying or working." His eyes glistened. "But I feel like playing again. I have missed it," he added, reaching into his pocket for a scrap of paper. "Do you have a pen?" he asked, careful not to appear too eager.

Brook picked up a pencil on the coffee table next to her and passed it to him, her hand lightly brushing his.

"Here's my phone number and address," he said, handing her the slip of paper, his cheeks reddening as the tips of his fingers rested momentarily on her wrist. "May I have yours? Maybe we could get together sometime and play music."

"Really? Do you think we could?" she asked, her eyes wide at the anticipation of such a pleasure. They could both hear her husband in the background, making small talk with Plum. Brook's eyes dimmed. As she lowered her gaze, she whispered a verse by an ancient Chinese poet: "The flowers are gone with the stream, and the spring is over."

"But an earthly paradise never disappears," Rain said undeterred, reciting a verse from another classic poem, which took Brook by surprise, eliciting an appreciative smile.

"Mommy!" Jimmy, Brooke's son, cried out as he ran out of his bedroom. "I want Donald Duck!" He climbed into his mother's lap. Brook cradled him in her arms, distracted, her eyes lingering on Rain's face.

Green years fly by. Nobody can stop time. Is love in my dream? Or am I dreaming love? Rain thought of this verse as he watched Brook hold her son. He was about to recite it when Den and Plum returned to the living room.

"Let's get to know each other," Den said magnanimously. "Please, stay for dinner. We can talk about the old days, about back home." But Plum was quick to respond that she and Rain unfortunately had other plans for the evening.

***

Later, after grabbing a burger at McDonald's, Rain and Plum went to a revue cinema to see an old movie – *Ghost* – that Plum had loved. Plum watched the heart-warming story again with tears in her eyes, but all Rain could see was Brook. He couldn't shake her face from his mind.

They spent the night together in Rain's apartment. Lying in bed, Plum pulled Rain to her. He caressed her smooth body with his hands. But his thoughts were elsewhere. Two images of Brook haunted him. One was from eight years earlier – Brook playing the zither, her long braids dangling two bright red butterflies at their ends. The other was of her cradling her son in her arms earlier that day. Her concerned eyes had quickened his heartbeat.

"What's the matter?" asked Plum, shaking her hands in front of Rain's eyes in an effort to bring him back to the present.

Rain stretched his body over hers. *Forgetting is impossible. Sentiments always remain the same.* The lines from another classic Chinese poem popped into his head, and his heart throbbed. Lost in thoughts mixed with poetry and images of Brook, Rain sighed.

Disappointed, Plum pushed him away and climbed out of the bed.

***

The night after Rain's visit, Brook had trouble falling asleep. Whenever she closed her eyes, she pictured Rain's face. She felt as if his eyes were moving over her, touching her face, heart, and body. The melody of "The Moonlight" on clarinet resounded in her mind.

The following morning, Brook resumed her routine by cleaning up the house after Den went to work and her daughter left for school. After she had her son busy with his favourite toys, she pulled the zither case out from a stack in the storage room. Opening the case carefully, she noticed two of the strings on the zither were broken. She changed the strings and tried to tune them but failed to get the right sounds. She suddenly felt incapable. It was as if, after being speechless for years, and given the opportunity, suddenly, to speak, she did not have the words. Struggling with the pick, Brook played the zither but was unable to complete a composition. She realized that the melodies of several ancient Chinese compositions, such as "Grand North Tribes" and "Phoenix with One Hundred Birds," like precious pearls, had slid off her necklace and vanished into a bottomless sea. Could she get them back?

"Mommy!" wailed her son, whose finger was pinched between two Lego blocks.

Brook got up and went over to soothe him. Gently massaging his finger, she felt tears spill from her eyes. *What's the matter with me?*

In the succeeding days, a pair of eyes that resembled deep wells followed her everywhere. One afternoon, hesitating for only a moment, she dialled Rain's phone number. Her heart was racing, and the receiver dropped from her hand before she had pressed the last digit. She lost the courage to resume the call though she knew those two wells would follow her for the rest of her life.

In her dreams, pink blossoms fell off cherry trees in February, carpeting a pathway. As she wandered on that pathway through a moonlit field, the wind blew with the scent of rank petals. Two startled magpies swooped from the trees and disappeared into the night sky. She roamed, sometimes moving quickly, sometimes stumbling. She opened her arms, attempting to grasp at something and almost fell into a running river that suddenly emerged in front of her. Before closing her eyes, she spied a comet fly toward her. When it struck her, she woke from the dream with her arms outstretched to her husband beside her. He pulled her in his arms, his body nestled against hers, but she was restless and felt only the water from those two wells spilling over her body.

***

Rain had felt lost since he met Brook, especially during the lingering rains of March.

After work one Friday afternoon, Rain went to chauffeur Plum around to various stores, finally dropping her off at her favourite shop. On his way to pick her up, he fiddled with the radio dial in his car and was pleasantly surprised to come upon a channel that was broadcasting some of his favourite Chinese instrumentals: "Spring River and Flowers in the Moonlight" and "Joyful South Yangtze." He lost himself in the music until he finally pulled over and looked for Plum. He was astonished to find that he had parked in front of Brook's house. His heart in his throat, he restarted the car and hastily turned around.

When he finally arrived at the place where he had agreed to pick Plum up, he spotted her sitting on a bench at the far edge of the parking lot. He parked his car and strode purposely toward her, but she turned her head away. "Plum!" he called but did not hear her response. He reached her and touched her shoulder. "Sorry, I'm late," he mumbled.

Plum angrily pushed his hand away. "If I knew you were going to be late, I would've accepted a ride in someone else's car."

"All right," he distorted his mouth with a smile. "Go right ahead. There's a man about to get into a Toyota. Why not join him?" His throat tightened.

Plum raised her head, glaring at him. She ignored his comment. "How dare you leave me here waiting! You must be on time!"

"Are we going to Chinatown?" answered Rain, releasing a breath. He was too tired to fight.

"Of course, but…" She noticed his fatigue and hesitated. "I'd also like to go to the Manhattan Mall, if you don't mind. There are some new clothing stores I want to check out."

"Chinatown, then the Manhattan Mall? No problem," he responded in what he hoped was a valiant tone.

Twenty minutes later, Rain parked his car along Worth Street. While Plum went into a grocery store to pick up food for later, Rain went into

Chinatown's largest Chinese bookstore and gift shop. There he scoured the shelves for music. Finally, he found what he was looking for – a few cassettes of traditional Chinese music. He was especially pleased to discover a cassette of folk songs from Northwestern China. Rain smiled as he paid for the music, and kept smiling as he walked over to the grocery store. He met Plum at the checkout and helped her carry the packages out to the car. "Do you mind if we just go somewhere to grab a pizza?" he asked.

"What? Didn't we talk about having supper at my place?" A look of displeasure appeared on Plum's face. "I just bought all this stuff, and you know my housemate is away, and we…"

"It's just that I picked up a couple of great tapes of Chinese music and I really want to enjoy them tonight."

"What is it, Rain? You're so absentminded recently," Plum said. "It seems like you don't care about our plans or my feelings…"

"I'm tired," Rain interrupted her. "We can cook a meal next time. Come on. Let's go to the Manhattan Mall now." He walked so fast back to the parking lot that Plum had to hurry after him.

In the fitting room at the Dragon Lady Fine Clothing store, Plum tried on several different dresses. She adored a lemon yellow V-necked dress with a wide, black belt. With it on, she went to show Rain, who was waiting at the counter. "You look great," he said.

"Really?" She whirled around, the silk dress outlining her plump breasts and curvy figure. The silky fabric shimmered under the shop's pleasant light.

"You know it does," he grinned. "You don't need to ask."

"Okay, I'll take it." She returned to the fitting room to change, while Rain paid for the dress. Plum was all smiles as she carried the shopping bag with her new dress out of the mall.

On their way home, Plum looked out the window at the street's neon lights drizzling blue, pink, and white. She imagined her gorgeous figure in the new dress drifting through the crowd.

Rain's eyes were fixed on the road ahead of him, and except for the changing traffic lights, all he could focus on was the rainy, gloomy sky. In this silent world, he heard his heart sigh. *Does she want to see me like I want to see her?*

***

Weeks later, Brook was rummaging in a kitchen cabinet and found a package of leftover ginkgo nuts, a main ingredient for her sweet summer soup. A memory filled her as she gazed at the cream-coloured, lima-bean-sized nuts. As a child, whenever she saw a street vendor selling fried ginkgo nuts she begged her mother to join the line. She watched the metal spatula go up and down into the huge wok and listened to it clank. When she clutched her package of warm nuts, she forgot her sore legs as they made their way home.

Several years later, during the Cultural Revolution, she was sent to the countryside like other students. She moved to a village called Dragon Valley, which had a hundred-year-old ginkgo tree. It was a female, but her delicate blossoms never bore fruit as there were no male trees nearby. In the fall, the fan-shaped leaves swirled onto the ground settling into layers that resembled a yellow rug. Brook loved the shape of the leaves and always picked some as they reminded her of home and her childhood.

One summer evening, Brook carried two bundles of wheat from the field to the barnyard as the last task of her daily chores. When she staggered past the gingko tree, her stomach cramped. She stopped under the tree and sat on one of her bundles. Alone in the dusk, holding her stomach, she felt helpless. A group of crows flew over her head, and she groaned. The pain lessened a bit, and as dusk turned to darkness, she dozed off on her bundle.

"Hey there! What's wrong?"

She awoke to find a young man from the next village standing above her. "I ... I have a stomachache," she stuttered.

"Can you move? I can carry your bundles," said the young man. She attempted to rise but failed.

"I'll carry you home. You look like you're really under the weather."

"No. I'll wait a while. I'll be okay."

"Wait? I don't think so. It's dark. Let me take you home." He helped her up. "Tell me where you live," he insisted politely.

Finally, Brook agreed and let him carry her home.

His name was Lu. He was also a student who had been sent from the city to the country for Mao's "re-education" program. They became fast friends and soon were inseparable. He had many books of literature to share with her, which fascinated Brook and opened a window to a wider world. The books escorted her through many evenings, joined her with Lu, and buoyed both their hopes. She imagined going to university, and he dreamed of being a war reporter like Ernest Hemingway.

One day, their commune began recruiting young men for Mao's army. Lu asked her, "Do you think I should apply?"

"Why not?" answered Brook, though a sense of loss shrivelled her heart. Joining the army was expected for the young men in the countryside and would guarantee a good job in the future.

"If you want me to stay, I won't go," he said, his eyes searching her face for a glimmer of hope.

But she did not say anything, so Lu joined the army.

Before he left, they met under the ginkgo tree. He hugged her, his lips seeking hers. When her body weakened against his, she knew she loved him. Gently she pushed his head away. Under Mao, youthful love affairs were a sign of a corrupt lifestyle. In her mind, affection between a man and woman was purely spiritual, and physical desire seemed out of place somehow.

It was several years before she returned to the city. She had not stopped thinking about Lu, and regretted that she had not tried to keep him from joining the army. Working hard to survive, she kept hoping for a miracle, hoping that Lu might one day come looking for her. She believed that love was a rainbow that would appear at the right time and she felt ready now. Many times, she dreamed of the ginkgo tree in the Dragon Valley. In her dreams, thousands of yellow ginkgo leaves swirled with the wind, blanketing the entire village, but she never saw another human figure in those dreams, let alone Lu. Each time she woke, she felt lost in the past.

***

Now, the package of ginkgo nuts awakened her desire for something more. How had she missed her chance at a life with Lu, someone she had loved deeply? Holding the nuts in her hand, she suddenly thought: *Maybe these ginkgo nuts will grow, and I won't miss anything more in my life.*

She carried all the nuts to the garden outside her house and buried them in the soil underneath the windows. As she watered the earth that covered the ginkgo nuts, she felt herself become a child again. Like sunshine, a smile danced on her face, and she took delight in sowing her dream seeds.

Brook watered her garden constantly and watched daily for any change. Daffodils, tulips, and irises bloomed in turn, and soon other plants and shrubs sported shiny new leaves and branches. But nothing happened in the soil that held the ginkgo nuts.

***

One Saturday evening, Rain lay in bed, listening to the northwestern Chinese folk songs on the cassette that had become his favourite. The words of a song echoed in the room, taunting him:

A young singer arises from the mountains
Nobody has ever heard his voice
The yellow land wakes from slumber
The currents of rivers echo his thoughts

In a wink, thousands of years pass
The universe is still speechless
Raindrops can make a loud noise
The young man has broken the silence

Rain pictured himself climbing up an eighteen-storey crystal tower. Once on top, a glittering river appeared below him like a graceful green ribbon dotted with red, blue, yellow and white sails flowing languorously like the melody that washed over him in his sleep. Suddenly, he felt his arms become tense and hair sprout from his skin. Soon, he was covered with white feathers. He pinched his ear, and it ached. *I'm not in a dream,* he told himself.

"Fly! Fly into the sky. Fly toward the sun." The words of a song from his childhood arose.

"Rain! Wait up! I want to fly…" He heard Brook's voice. "My ginkgo nuts have sprouted!"

He gripped Brook's arm and together they sprang into the sky, the crystal tower collapsing below them. Thousands of sparkling pieces of glass flew into the air, then plunged to the ground. Rain rolled over in bed, abruptly falling onto the carpet. In his dream, he was still clinging to Brook's arm, telling her, "I want to see your ginkgo trees."

Rain sat up on the floor, pondering his dream. He did not understand why he dreamt about Brook, but he did remember she had ordered ginkgo nut soup in the Red Bean Teahouse those many years ago.

He climbed back into bed, but could not get back to sleep. It was then that he resolved to phone her as soon as possible.

After breakfast, Rain dialled Brook's phone number. To his surprise, he heard an elderly woman's voice on the line. *She has a guest*, he thought and asked, "May I speak to Brook?"

"Yeah … *oh, nah!*" The woman exhaled. "Who's calling?"

"Rain. Is Brook in?" Impatience and anxiety arose in him.

"No, she … she is…," quavered the woman.

"What's happened?" he asked, his voice weak, his other hand twisting the phone cord around his wrist.

"A car accident …," the woman sobbed. "She is gone."

Rain's hand gripped the phone so hard that it hurt.

"Her husband's still at the hospital. I'm here taking care of …"

Before she could finish, Rain hung up the phone and slumped into the nearest chair. He was flooded with pain, as if he had been stabbed in the heart. He moaned softly, his hands clasping his head.

He had waited too long to phone, too long to tell her how he really felt. He had missed his chance, again. When Plum walked into the room, he asked her if she thought ginkgo trees could grow in New York.

FORTUNE-TELLING

S HE FEELS LESS DIZZY AFTER shambling out of the smoke-filled office into the waiting room with one hand on her forehead.

"Are you okay, Lin?" asks her friend, Joyce, who sits in an armchair and looks at her with concern.

"Not really. It was strange," Lin responds and plops down in another armchair.

"Joyce Parry!" calls out the receptionist at the counter.

Joyce stands up and walks toward the adjoining office.

Under her breath, Lin says, "Good luck!"

Lin stretches out her arms. This is almost the same as fortune-telling in China. *Twice, the fortune-teller said I had an ex-lover who had been difficult, dominating. Was he just guessing?* A few days ago, Lin saw an ad for fortune-telling on a bulletin board outside her dorm room and felt curious about it. She had asked Joyce if she had ever been to a fortune-teller.

"No," answered Joyce. "But a friend of mine went to this fortune-teller who advertises around campus, and she said he was great. Do you want to go? Next week is reading week. Let's go, just for fun!"

This is how they end up in this room.

Lin met Joyce a year before in a psychology class. Joyce majors in social work, and Lin majors in math. Few of their classes overlap, but since meeting, they have tried to take some of their elective courses together. They both live on campus and often meet in the computer lab to do research or work on their assignments.

One night Lin worked in the lab until midnight. When she was about to leave, Joyce asked, "Would you mind waiting for me for just a couple of minutes? I'll be finished soon."

"Are you afraid of the dark?" Lin joked on their way to their dorm rooms.

"Not that," she said, "but men. Last night this guy and I were left in the lab. He wanted to chat with me, saying he would wait for me till I finished my assignment."

"Was he friendly?"

"Overly friendly. He asked me which dorm I lived in and wanted to walk me back to my room. That really scared me. I made an excuse, saying that I needed to go to the washroom."

"Then what happened?" asked Lin.

"I made like I was going into the washroom, then took an elevator upstairs and left through another exit. I ran all the way back to my dorm. I was afraid he would show up tonight."

Since then, Lin and Joyce have always left the computer lab together at night. Sometimes they hold each other's hand when they walk along the alley through the dim-lit area.

***

Lin picks up a back issue of *Canadian Living* from the coffee table and flips the pages. She glances at an advertisement for Olay skincare. That's the product I use, she thinks, tossing the magazine back onto the table. After selecting another glossy magazine, *Fashion*, she leafs through the pages, catching a glimpse of a bold title that reads, "Change Your Hair Colour as Often as You Wish," and features a sleek background of red, orange, blonde, silver, and black heads. She fingers her long hair, and tilts her head to look at the page. *Black is definitely a beautiful colour,* she tells herself. She has no interest in colouring her hair.

On another page, she discovers a short article entitled, "Special Exercises for Your Breasts," with several photos of women modelling various types of bras. It reminds her of her fussy boyfriend, who used to care a lot about the way she dressed and made herself up. He wanted her to dress up wherever they went. Chinese etiquette for women states: "Obey your father before you grow up, and obey your husband after you get married." So, she used to dress up and wear makeup just to please him. He became insufferable, but she put up with him because her parents preached that a virtuous girl did not change boyfriends. She even got a job in a daycare because her mother said it was excellent practice for motherhood.

After years of passive obedience, she suddenly woke up. Instead of rebelling as a teenager, she rebelled as an adult. She did not care about clothing, or makeup, or motherhood anymore. She left her boyfriend and enrolled in a university away from home, majoring in mathematics. She wanted to prove to her parents that not only could girls learn math, but they could also teach math.

When she broke with her ex, he'd said, "You'll regret it." Sometimes Lin asks herself: *Do I regret leaving him?* Her answer is always no. She feels only relief that he is out of her life. Away from him and away from her parents, she lives the way she prefers and pursues what she wants.

***

She hears Joyce's cheerful voice as she emerges from the other room. "Let's go home," she says, walking to the coat rack.

"How was it?" asks Lin.

"Hang on. I'll tell you in the car."

Placing the magazine onto the coffee table, Lin rises and grabs her coat from the rack. Pulling it over her shoulders, she follows Joyce out of the building. It has stopped snowing, and everything around them looks fluffy and white. The sunset colours the surface of the snow with crimson beams.

They climb into Joyce's car. Joyce holds the steering wheel with one hand and shifts the gears with the other. When the car starts to move, Joyce asks, "Did you think he could see into your past?"

"I don't think so. He asked me if I had received a college education since I seemed so smart. But I didn't answer him," says Lin with a sense of triumph. "When he wanted to know whether I was married, I told him to guess. He definitely had trouble guessing things right."

"Why would you do that?" Joyce glances at Lin and raises her eyebrows. "How can he foretell things for you if you don't co-operate?"

"I think a fortune-teller is supposed to just know things. What kind of fortune-teller has to ask his clients for information?"

"Like a psychiatrist, he needs to talk with you and analyze your situation. Then he can trace your past and define tendencies in your life," explains Joyce with patience. "He read me very well. He told me right away that I hated my father and feared men. He even knew I'd experienced something severely painful."

"Severely painful?"

Joyce nods. "It was my first experience with a man. The fortune-teller drew a human figure on the table with a piece of chalk when he spoke to me. Staring intently at the Tarot card I'd pulled from the deck in his hand and given to him, he moved his finger around the sketch. I think he was trying to match what he'd read from the card with his diagram on the table. Finally his hand paused beneath the figure's abdomen. Then, he asked me, 'Were you in too much pain to speak at that time?' I think he must have sensed the pain I'd felt ten years earlier with my boyfriend at the time. I didn't want to have sex with him and he got a little rough with me. I broke up with him afterwards."

Lin nods with what she hopes is a comforting smile on her face. "Would it be okay for me to ask why you hate your father?" she asks.

Joyce is silent for just a moment. "He raped my mother when she was only fifteen years old. At that time he was already in his fifties…" Joyce's hands tremble and the car abruptly shifts, crossing the road's yellow line before veering back. "I was sent to an orphanage after my birth. That's where I spent the first years of life, before I was finally adopted."

"How do you know this?" asks Lin under her breath.

"My adoptive mother told me about the orphanage and where I could find it. As an adult, I went back and they gave me information about my background."

"Have you found your parents? I mean, your mother."

"Yes. My mother's married, and has two other kids. My father was arrested and put behind bars. He died in a nursing home many years later. Every once in a while, I thought of going to see him, but I didn't have the courage…" Her voice starts to quaver.

"I can't imagine how painful that must have been for you."

"I hate my father because he both created and destroyed my life at the same time. I'm his blood, but he's my shame. And it is because of him that I can't be with a man. Thinking of him just makes me feel sick. I really…"

The car starts to weave again. Lin feels Joyce's anger, and knows that she is no longer focusing on the road. She tries to calm her down. "There's a gas station ahead. Maybe we should stop –"

Lin does not have time to finish her sentence. A car is coming straight for them. Joyce's hands shake on the steering wheel. Lin grabs the wheel from her and steers toward the road's shoulder, narrowly missing a head-on collision.

The car hurtles over an embankment. Lin is thrown against the window and then back against her seat. When the car lands with a thunderclap at the bottom of the ditch, she loses consciousness.

Lin feels as though she were floating in the endless, black sky. A gentle touch makes her sense warmth. She opens her eyes slowly and finds herself in Joyce's arms. She utters, "Yong, where are we?"

"We're in the ditch, Lin. The car is wrecked, but you saved our lives." Joyce's soft voice resounds in her ear. "We've got to go get help from the gas station, get them to tow the car out of the ditch." Joyce's voice strains with concern, but she manages a weak smile. "Lin, are you okay? Who's Yong?"

Lin shakes her head. She is confused and rattles. "Yong ? Did I say Yong?" Her face flushes. "He's my ex-boyfriend."

The fortune-teller's words suddenly come back to her, "Your lover is nearby and is waiting for you." *What did the fortune-teller mean? A lover nearby?*

The scene of rainbow flags floating over the heads of people marching along the path winding up Citadel Hill flashes in her mind. The parade was earlier that summer. She and Joyce watched the parade from the sidewalk that was crammed with spectators. "Let's walk with them," Joyce said on the spur of the moment. Grabbing Lin's hand, Joyce pulled Lin seamlessly into the middle of the parade. They were welcomed by a group of women chanting and singing in unison as they waved a bright pink flag in their hands.

Lin's face feels hot. She is conscious of the warmth of Joyce's body enveloping her. Raising her fingers to her head, Lin traces the small scratches on the side of her cheek. She stammers, "I … I need to see the fortune-teller again."

Surprised, Joyce asks, "Why?" She strokes Lin's back lightly. "I don't want any more fortune-telling. I think a person's fate is destined at birth."

Lin sighs and leans her head on Joyce's shoulder, aware of the sweet fragrance of her hair. She is surprised to hear herself murmur, "I wonder if I can find happiness here, in this new place."

"I know you can. *We* can." Joyce says, running her fingers slowly through Lin's hair. "Let's get going. I'm thankful neither one of us is seriously hurt."

They help each other climb out of the car. Dusk has fallen. The gas station looks like a tight handful of stars glowing, just ahead of them. They make their way towards the station with hope, hand in hand. The streetlights turn on, casting their washed-out light on the snow-covered road. The two shadows merge into one as they move toward the lit oasis.

LIFE INSURANCE

MEILI FELT EXHILARATED AS SHE flipped through the brochure. On the front page, the words in Chinese read, "Moon Life Insurance." She picked up a telephone book from the shelf and sat down at the table. *So far so good.* She took a deep breath. *I can earn money from home now.*

Beginning at the "A's", she stared at the very first page, searching out names that sounded Chinese. She found one and then pressed the numbers on her push-button phone. "Mr. An, how do you do? I'm calling from the Moon Life Insurance Company."

"Don't understand your language. Sorry." The other person hung up.

She punched in another phone number. "Hi, Mrs. Ai."

"Speaking."

"I'm from the Moon Life…"

"Sorry. I don't need any insurance."

"Let me explain…" The woman hung up before Meili could finish her sentence.

Meili started to worry. *This isn't as easy as I expected.* She sat still for a moment at the table though her hand could not help but turn over the phone book. When her eyes fixed on the last page, she suddenly thought, *Why not start at the end?*

She punched in one phone number, then another. Her finger began to ache, and her tongue became numb.

Later that afternoon, Meili finally reached an elderly woman who showed some interest in the insurance plan and asked her to come over with more details. They made an appointment for 5:00 p.m.

Meili put on makeup, and then dressed in business clothes. She looked at herself in a full-length mirror, and approved of her slender figure in the dark brown suit. Gold earrings glittered under her bobbed black hair, but she had dark circles under her eyes. *Oh, who cares? The old lady won't even notice,* she thought.

Twenty minutes later, Meili hurried away from the Eglinton subway station and walked east for about ten minutes. Finally she saw a house with a cherry tree full of red fruit in the front yard and the number 222 engraved on the brass plate that hung on the front door. Meili took a deep breath and glanced at her watch – 4:43 p.m.

To her surprise, the door opened before she even had time to knock, and a woman with short, silver hair squinted at her as she held the door slightly ajar.

"Come on in. I'm the person you are visiting," said the elderly woman, smiling at Meili.

"Mrs. Yang. Nice to meet you."

"Likewise." The woman led Meili to a large armchair in the living room. After motioning for her to sit down, Mrs. Yang sank onto the couch next to the chair and said, "So, tell me what you are selling."

"My company has an excellent life insurance plan." Meili took out a booklet from her bag and read it to Mrs. Yang. "Guarantees at maturity and death with our segregated funds. Easy savings through automatic monthly deposits…"

"I'm sorry to interrupt you. Can you explain this to me in Chinese?"

"Of course." Meili began speaking Chinese, which loosened her tongue. She described the policy as clearly as possible although "life insurance" was new jargon to her. It sounded like something to help people live longer. All Meili needed was to live well without worrying about life. She wondered what would insure a life free from uncertainty.

"Okay, I'll take it," the woman announced emphatically.

"Really? That's great!" Meili was surprised. "I'll sign you up right away," she said with a delighted smile.

Mrs. Yang looked Meili up and down with interest, and then asked, "By the way, are you married?"

"No, not yet."

"You're young and will find a good husband." Mrs. Yang smiled again.

"What about you? Are you ... are you married?" asked Meili with curiosity.

"I'm widowed. My husband died young so I raised my son by myself. Luckily, I inherited enough money from my late husband to be able to do so comfortably. Now my son sends me ... money every month. He's a dutiful boy, very well-educated, and he has a good job..." Meili thought that perhaps Mrs. Yang had not talked to anyone for a long time and needed a listener.

"I'm so glad to talk to you," Mrs. Yang added. Meili thought Mrs. Yang must have read her mind. "Everybody else I know is busy with their own family." She gazed at Meili quizzically. "By the way, does your job bring you a lot of money?"

"Ha," Meili chuckled. "You're my first client. It's hard to get a customer. You know, not many people want life insurance."

"Like me, I don't – I mean, I have a job for you if you wish."

"A job?"

"I am looking for a companion," said Mrs. Yang. "Spend half a day with me just to chat. Sometimes, maybe, we could go shopping."

"Everyday?"

"No. Once a week is enough. I'll pay you fifty dollars each time you come."

"Sure," said Meili, sure that luck had finally found her. "I would really like to do this. Thanks." She was elated. Chatting and keeping an elderly woman company seemed easier than babysitting for her sister. Unless she had the good fortune to get many more clients like Mrs. Yang, Meili felt fairly certain that working for Moon Life Insurance wasn't going to even pay the rent.

"Which day do you need me?" asked Meili.

"How about every Saturday afternoon?"

"That's fine with me."

***

For the past three and half years, Meili had been living with her sister's family and helped look after her niece on weekends as the little girl went to daycare during the week. It looked like meeting Mrs. Yang would help her escape babysitting on Saturdays. *Why not?* Meili needed to find her own niche in life, instead of depending on her sister. She wondered, *Should I stand on my own two feet or try to find a husband I can depend on?* She imagined and hoped for a happy life, complete with a worry-free future, just like anyone who bought a life insurance policy.

One Saturday, having spent the afternoon with Mrs. Yang, Meili returned to her sister's home. When she opened the door and smelled dinner, she felt hungry and rushed through the living room to the kitchen.

"Meili, your food's on the counter. We could only wait until six," said Suli, her sister, who was watching TV in the living room.

"That's okay." Meili hung her handbag on the back of a chair. Then she took a bowl and chopsticks, and sat at the kitchen table to eat her supper.

After Meili had washed the dinner dishes, Suli joined her in the kitchen. "How's your job going?"

"Which one?"

"With Mrs. Yang."

"So far so good. It's easy. We spend most of the time just talking."

"Interesting. I wonder why she would hire someone just to chat with her."

"I guess because she's lonely and needs a companion."

"You said she has a son. Does her son have a family or children?"

"Her son lives in Montreal. Children? He isn't even married. How can he have any children?"

"Ha," Suli laughed. "You don't know enough about this country."

"What?" Meili disliked her tone, and her eyebrows went up. "I don't know about this country because all I've done is stay home and take care of your kid…"

"Whoa! Enough. You only babysit once a week now!" Suli frowned and changed the topic. "Do you enjoy selling life insurance policies?"

"Yes, but so far I've only sold one policy."

"Keep trying. You might get lucky." Suli hesitated for a minute then said, "Maybe you should start looking for a man. You don't want to be living with me forever."

"I'll try my luck. But, sis," grumbled Meili. "I don't need a mother hen."

Before her sister could answer, Meili took her handbag and left the kitchen for her bedroom. After she relaxed on the bed, with pillows surrounding her, Meili drew a newspaper out of her bag and searched the ads under Personals and Friends. She finally focused on an ad that read: "A successful and professional businessman in his late thirties is interested in a long-term, committed relationship. Would like to meet someone who is an attractive Asian or Caucasian woman between 28- 35 years old living in Canada."

Meili sat up. *I'm the right person! A twenty-nine-year-old Chinese woman, smart, slim, and interesting.* After examining the ad again, she got up to look for scissors. With excitement, she cut out the ad from the paper and copied down the phone number in her notebook. *I'll call as soon as possible.* She almost shouted: *My luck is just around the corner!*

***

Two weeks later, after setting up a date with the businessman whose ad she had seen in the personals, Meili decided to tell her sister about her plan.

"Sis, will you come to my room?" asked Meili after they had finished dinner and tidied the kitchen.

"Sure," answered Suli, who left her daughter and her husband to watch *Lion King* and followed Meili into her room. "What's new?"

"I just wanted to let you know I'm going to meet a man," said Meili, sitting on the edge of her bed.

"A man! You didn't tell me −" Suli caught her breath. "Okay, who is he?"

"A businessman. His name is Linqi."

"Linqi? That's a strange name... Is he in Toronto?"

"No. I'll be meeting him in Ottawa."

"What? Does he work in Ottawa?"

"No, he works in Moncton."

"Are you crazy? You're going to meet a man in Ottawa, where you don't know anybody, or him, for that matter! Why didn't you ask him to come to Toronto?"

"He said he had to take a longer trip than me to reach Ottawa. I think it's only fair for me to meet him part-way."

"Right, you already put yourself in his shoes. You must really like him." Suli said sarcastically, clapping her hands as though cheering on a wonderful performance. "Great! A blind romance! When are you going?"

"Next Thursday. I'll take a train and come back the following day…" Meili hesitated. "Do you think it's a bad idea?"

"Bad idea?" Suli smirked. "You won't listen to me…"

"Am I too old?" Meili became anxious.

"Too old? How old is he?"

"In his thirties, I guess. He's at least thirty-five."

"You're not old! You're a couple of years younger. The problem is blind dates can be dangerous, especially for girls. And it isn't the Chinese way, you know. Some men may only want to take advantage of you. You're really going overboard, to date a man you've never seen, in a city you've never ever been to, and he doesn't even live in! Would any other normal Chinese girl be as bold as you?"

"I'm old enough, sister!" Meili rolled her eyes. She got up off the bed and turned her back to Suli, tapping her foot on the floor to indicate her impatience.

"Okay, I won't say anything, but you need to be careful. Don't trust–" Suli halted as soon as Meili turned back around, her eyes downcast. "I can lend you any dress or skirt you like. And I'll give you $100 to help with your trip."

Meili brightened and said, "Thanks, Suli. Wish me good luck."

Suli sighed. "Of course … I hope it all goes well."

That night, Meili had a dream: she wandered down an empty street looking for someone to ask for directions. A girl walked past her. Excited, she asked, "Excuse me. Could you please tell me where Pacific Mall is?"

"Pacific Mall? Do you mean Pacific Ocean?"

Meili shook her head. "No, I mean 'Pacific Mall.'"

"I don't understand," the girl said with a confused look. "Sorry. I can't help." She left.

Meili realized she was speaking Chinese. She tried to speak English but could not make any sound. At that moment, she saw a huge building not far from the street. She recognized it as the mall she had been looking for. When she entered the mall, she saw crowds of people moving about. She bought a pink polka-dotted dress from an Italian fashion store. When she left the building, the streetlights were on. They glimmered and smiled around her, sweet and warm.

The next morning, Meili felt gorgeous. Looking out the window of her sister's tenth floor apartment, Meili's eyes drank in the red and gold maple trees dotting green lawns like colourful balloons. She imagined that some day she would sit on the porch of a beautiful house, and watch her children chase butterflies around the maple trees on the front lawn.

She decided to get her hair dyed in order to impress her date. In the afternoon, she would flip through the pages of the "H's" in the telephone directory to hunt for more potential clients.

***

Her train arrived in Ottawa in the early afternoon. She stood up from her seat and smoothed her pink dress that she had borrowed from her sister. With a mini-suitcase in her hand, she strolled toward a turnstile. She glanced around the station and saw several men. *Which one is he?* Only two men wore T-shirts. The younger one's T-shirt had a picture of a white sailboat. *It must be him!* He had told her he loved sailing. Her eyes beamed as the man smiled and walked toward her. "I'm Linqi. Are you Meili?"

Glad to be recognized, Meili nodded. "How did you know?"

"Well, I wasn't sure, but you looked like you were waiting for someone." Linqi's gaze fell on her hair, which she had just dyed blond. He had expected to see a black-haired girl. He stretched out his hand. "May I carry your suitcase?"

"You don't have to," she answered as she handed him the suitcase and then followed him out of the station. "Where are we going?"

"Do you mind going to my hotel? I have already reserved a room." He looked at her and waited for a gesture of consent. "We can leave your suitcase there and go out."

"Okay, I'll check into the same hotel." She paused at a parking meter, wondering where the hotel was.

"All right, let's go." Linqi turned and beckoned for a taxi.

The taxi took them to a Holiday Inn and stopped in front of the entrance. Linqi paid the driver, got out, and opened the door for Meili. They entered the lobby. After a discussion with the desk clerk, Meili received a key to a room, which was on the same floor as Linqi's.

"Would you like to take a walk outside or have a rest first?" asked Linqi once they reached her room.

"I'm not tired. We can walk if you want to," answered Meili as she opened the door to her room and stepped inside to deposit her suitcase. She was eager to get to know him, but did not know where to begin. *Maybe I should just go along with what he feels like doing*, she thought. Under her breath, she mouthed, "A guest will follow a host. You can decide what to do –"

"We're guests to each other," he said to her, smiling as if he had read her mind. "So you can decide and I'll follow you. By the way, have you ever visited Ottawa before?"

Meili shook her head. "I'd like to visit Parliament Hill if that's okay." Suddenly, she remembered something. "Linqi, do you mind if I make a phone call?"

"Not at all. Do you know anyone in Ottawa?"

"No. I need to call my sister in Toronto." She motioned for Linqi to come into the room. Up to this point, he had remained standing in the doorway. She walked to the window and took her cell phone out of her purse. Linqi sat in the only armchair in the room, while Meili dialled Suli's number and gave her the name and phone number of the hotel she had checked into.

Linqi waited until she finished her call. "I know the city well because I once studied at a university here. I can be your guide." Rising from the chair, he walked over to her and pointed through the window at a green-roofed tower in the distance. "See that green pointy roof? That's Parliament Hill. It's about a twenty-minute walk from here or a couple of minutes by bus or taxi. Which way do you prefer?"

"On foot, of course." *Walking will provide us with a better way to get to know each other.*

After they visited Parliament Hill, Linqi suggested they eat at a Swiss Chalet. Meili did not enjoy non-Chinese food, but showed her respect for his choice. She kept telling herself, *I can learn and adapt.* She ordered what he ordered even though she had a problem with salad. She stared at the raw lettuce, green pepper, and onion on the plate, frowning. *How can I eat this?* She poured a lot of French dressing on the vegetables before biting into them.

"It's sour, isn't it?" Linqi noticed her twisted face and said, "You could leave the salad if you don't like it. It took me half a year to get used to North American food."

"After twenty years in the States and Canada, which food have you eaten the most?" Meili gave up on the salad and took a bite of her quarter chicken.

"Any food that is served fast. Apparently you aren't used to fast food yet." Linqi chewed the chicken, and his lips glistened under the lights when he spoke. "Do you like your job?"

"Well, it's hard to get customers. I've only found three in two months," answered Meili. "Do you have a family here?" Looking into Linqi's puzzled eyes, she added, "I mean parents and siblings."

"No, I only have an aunt. I'm a lone wolf," Linqi smirked.

"Are you hunting sheep?" Meili giggled. *It's a good thing,* she thought, *that he doesn't have parents to look after.*

"What?" Linqi stared into her face. "I meant that I've struggled all my life like a wolf. But I've gotten ahead."

"It's difficult for women."

"It's easier for women if they have higher education," he replied.

"Ah, but how could I afford it? Besides, my English is not good enough." Meili only had a high school diploma from China. Her babysitting job did not help her learn English, and her telemarketing job didn't make her enough money to cover tuition costs. Going to university was a mere daydream.

"Have you made the effort?" He took a napkin and cleaned his lips. "I worked hard although I could've had an easier life –"

"Do you…" Meili interrupted him and searched for the right words. "Did you have a lot of response to your personal ad?"

"I've met a couple of women. Have you ever had any boyfriends?" asked Linqi before he took a sip of his ice-cream shake.

"Not really." Meili drank her tea.

"Why not?"

"My sister introduced me to some university graduates, but I was not interested."

"Why are you interested in me?"

"You're handsome and successful…"

"You never saw me before today." Linqi laughed. "You're apparently interested in businessmen."

"You sounded all right to me when we spoke on the phone." Meili's face flushed. "Maybe you think I'm not good enough, but I can learn more English. I can do lots of things."

"That's good," Linqi nodded.

She relaxed a little. They ate in silence for a minute. Then she asked, "Do you have a good business?"

"Not bad. My company sells quality computer products. And I have a well-trained staff." Linqi breathed deeply and added, "But sometimes, I doubt if business is what I'm actually interested in. But, let's not talk about it, okay? I'm a businessman who hates business. Ha!"

Linqi looked naïve when he laughed, but his laughter made Meili uncomfortable. She did not know why.

***

The evening was pleasantly cool, and the scent of marigolds filled the air. Meili felt a little frustrated after supper when they strolled back to the Holiday Inn. *What does Linqi want? He's too sophisticated for me,* Meili sighed.

"Are you tired?" asked Linqi as they walked up to their floor.

"Not really." Meili motioned toward her room. "You can join me if you like."

"I'll walk you there."

"You…" Meili choked as she approached her door. Her voice began quivering. "You're not sincere. I thought you were interested in a serious relationship. Yet, you don't want to talk about your plans for the future although you know I'm serious." She entered the room and sank into the armchair.

"What plans? You mean a long-term relationship?"

"Yes, you know what I mean." Meili felt disappointed, and tears began to well up in her eyes.

"It's hard for me to promise you anything on the basis of a first date." Linqi walked to her and stood beside the chair, placing his hand on her shoulder. "You're a little bit too –"

"Too what?"

"I'm not sure. It's a little hard to catch on to what you mean. Maybe you think too much."

"You don't think, do you?" Meili took hold of his hand.

"I don't think when I date. I just want to have a good time."

"Can you have a good time forever?"

"Ah huh!" Linqi chuckled. "Is my mother here? I tried marriage before, but it didn't work."

"Do you want to see me again?"

Linqi sat down on the arm of the chair. His hand caressed her short hair that shone golden under the light. "Do you mind telling me why you've bleached your hair blond?"

"I like the colour. Why not?"

"I like the colour, too. But," he paused for a second and said, "I feel quite amused when I see a 'bottle blonde' who can't speak English or French well. I think learning the language and culture is more important than changing the colour of your hair."

"I'm learning English, too." Meili raised her head. "Tell me what I can do to please you?"

"There is something lovely in you." Linqi stood up. "Sleep well. I have an early meeting tomorrow morning and have to say goodbye to you now."

Meili's eyes dimmed, and her lips moved but did not say anything more.

He paused at the door. "By the way, Linqi is a pen name for the ad. My real name is Henry Ow Yang." It was as if he were able to guess her thoughts. He added, "I might call you up next Monday. If not, forget me. Good night."

That night, Meili dreamt that she had wandered into a forest and got lost. When she woke up, she realized she was in room at the Holiday Inn hotel and would take the train home to Toronto in the morning with an uninsured heart.

***

Saturday again and it was sunny. Meili returned home from the hair salon and looked into the mirror before going to meet with Mrs. Yang. Her hair appeared shiny and dark in the mirror's reflection. Remembering Mrs. Yang's habit of strolling in the park on fine days, Meili put on a dark red sweater and a pair of stone-washed jeans.

She arrived at Mrs. Yang's house as usual at one o'clock and walked into her living room.

"Take a seat. Let's drink some tea before going to the park." Mrs. Yang said as she placed a teapot on the table. "My son's back home."

"Your son? Where is he?" Meili looked around but did not see anyone else. She had heard Mrs. Yang talk about her son a few times. In Meili's mind, he was a boy of ten, which was the only photo of her son that she had seen. According to Mrs. Yang, parents in her hometown would never show recent photos of their only child to any person unknown to the child. This was a way for them to protect their child's soul from slipping away with strangers.

"He came home yesterday. He had to go to a meeting and will be back pretty soon."

"How old is he?" Meili became curious.

"He'll be thirty-eight this coming Monday. You know he's my only baby. I hope he can find a decent wife. Would you like to meet him, Meili? He's a wonderful boy."

Meili grinned at Mrs. Yang and thought, *You bought my insurance once before. Now you want to sell me your son. Who knows if a thirty-eight-year-old is really a wonderful boy?* "Sure, why not?"

At about 1:30 p.m., they heard footsteps approaching the front entrance. Mrs. Yang rose quickly from the couch and went to open the door. "Henry Ow, come meet Meili, my delightful companion."

"Meili?" a man stepped in and gaped at Meili, who had already stood up from her chair with a puzzled look as well.

Meili recognized him immediately. "Yes, it's me." She pointed to Mrs.

Yang. "Henry Ow, is this your mother or aunt?"

At that moment, Mrs. Yang clapped her hands with delight. "My dears, you've already met?"

"Is he your son or nephew?" asked Meili. "He lives in Moncton, not Montreal!"

"Yes. Isn't Moncton part of Montreal?" said Mrs. Yang. "In my home-town, a widow calls her only child 'nephew' and the child calls his mother 'aunt.' This is the way we widows used to have our children blessed. And this is why my son calls me 'aunt.'" Mrs. Yang became enthusiastic when talking about her son. "You see, my son's grown well and is –"

"Aunt, take a break. You're too excited." With a grin, Henry Ow walked toward Meili and said, "It's good to see you again. You look like yourself now."

"Really…" Meili stood motionless, amazed at the encounter.

"How about having dinner with me tonight?" Henry Ow extended his hand.

Meili gripped his hand, delighted. "Okay. After I come back from the park."

Then she turned around to Mrs. Yang. "Are you ready for a walk, Mrs. Yang? We can go now."

"Yes. Let's take a walk." Mrs. Yang nodded and walked toward the door.

Meili followed suit. The porch's wind chimes jingled with the breeze, and sparkled in the sunlight.

A smile smoothed away the wrinkles on Mrs. Yang's face as she turned to Meili. "You can ask my son to buy your insurance later."

JING AND THE CATERPILLAR

ON A JULY AFTERNOON IN 1971 in Guangzhou, China, four-year-old Jing ran out of her apartment building to join her playmates on the lawn. It was hot and humid, but the children had fun looking for sweet grass roots.

"Jing, come and look," a girl about five years old called out. She stood near a shrub, pointing to a branch.

Jing scampered over and took a look. "Yuck, a worm!"

A match-sized green worm was hunched on a leaf. The girl picked up a twig and waved it at the worm. "You little thing. Where are you going?"

"I think it's going home," said Jing.

"Nope. I think it's eating the leaf," answered a boy, joining them. He prodded the worm with a small stick to help it move onto another leaf.

"Look, there are a few more worms here. They've eaten up all these leaves," Jing said in excitement.

"We're worms; we need food, too." The little girl changed her voice into a high-pitched whisper. "You girls and boys eat candy and cookies. We eat leaves."

"Ha, ha, little worm, let me give you some food." Jing giggled and plucked a leaf to feed the chanting girl.

"Thanks, Jing, but a leaf isn't enough. I want candy," the girl laughed.

"Big worm, I have candy for you," said the boy, smiling as he handed a white grass root to the girl.

"Ha, good boy." The girl took it and placed it into her mouth. "It's so sweet. Thank you."

"Look, I've found more sweet grass." Jing squatted and pulled out a few sweet grass roots. "Try mine. They must taste sweet, too."

The children searched for more sweet grass roots and then watched the worms squiggling on the shrub again.

Gradually, Jing felt sick to her stomach. Her head began to spin. She lay down on the lawn and closed her eyes. She dreamt of a boundless, dark green forest. In it was a cabin. A biplane was hovering over the forest cabin, spreading a mass of fog. In the cabin a man sat at his desk in front of a typewriter. His fingers tapped the tiny keys. A woman with a basket pushed open the door and stepped in. Golden-yellow mushrooms filled her basket. The round basket then turned into a huge, blooming sunflower.

"Will, you must be hungry. I've picked some fresh chanterelles," said the woman.

"My story is almost done…" replied the man.

***

"Mom, Daddy!" Jing awoke finally, but she did not understand why she was in the hospital. "I wanna go home."

"Oh, my baby! We're going home soon," answered her mother, tears in her eyes.

A doctor entered the ward and spoke to Jing's father, "Your daughter's fine now. You can take her home."

Her father asked, "Could you please tell me why she fell ill?"

Hesitating for an instant, the doctor said, "It might be a case of food poisoning."

"Impossible," said her father, "I do research on plants. The chanterelle we eat is a high quality, edible mushroom."

"I can't be certain. We can't use the lab right now due to frequent power blackouts. Anyway, your daughter has recovered. But be careful about her food."

The summer was over and the mosquito population eventually

decreased. The tree and lawn insecticide sprayings in the city became fewer. Jing's father stood by the window wondering as he watched the pest controller walk away.

*****

That same autumn, William Watts, a writer of children's books, sat in his forest cabin in New Brunswick, Canada, reading a letter from Environment Canada.

"I can't believe my eyes, Sheila." William handed the letter to his wife. "It says there have been no observed or reported cases of illness among people here that could be attributed to the use of poison spray. They say fenitrothion is still the best product to use in curtailing the spread of spruce budworms."

William recalled his symptoms after recently falling ill. He disagreed with Environment Canada's conclusions. A few months before, out on a walk with his wife, he heard the spray plane humming in the air nearby. They fell sick that same day.

"Will, we should keep reporting on the incident, about what happened to us," said Sheila, who placed the letter on the table. She remembered the day their lungs became inflamed and their eyes burned. Meanwhile, their noses were runny from a bout of the flu.

"We won't stop," William responded. He could not believe that the fiddleheads they ate a few weeks ago were responsible for causing severe stomach pain, headaches, and dizziness. They had also felt restless and anxious.

William said, "In the 1950s, DDT was said to be harmless to humans. Without the publication of *Silent Spring* by Rachel Carson in 1962, chemists wouldn't have realized that modern insecticides have a harmful impact on human beings."

He picked up a magazine from a pile of journals on the table. "You've read this article discussing the use of DDT in Northern New Brunswick, right?"

Sheila nodded. "Yes. I remember that according to the studies, in the 1950s, 50 to 98 percent of young salmon were in danger, depending on the size of the fish and the manner of spraying. DDT was also thought to cause liver cancer."

"That's why phosphamidon replaced DDT in 1968." William took some paper clippings from a folder and scanned them. "Then fenitrothion took over because phosphamidon was less safe. How can anyone guarantee that fenitrothion isn't harmful to human beings?"

"You know, if we don't obey the laws of nature, our world will face some serious problems." Sheila pulled a bunch of papers out of the pile and sorted through them. "Here's the article."

"You're enlightening." William took hold of his wife's hand. "We should continue digging up more information about this. We don't want any children suffering from the effects of the spray."

"You could write a piece about it." Sheila nodded.

In November 1971, William's article, "You Are a Worm," was published in *The Mysterious East*. It challenged the existing conclusion that fenitrothion was not harmlful to humans.

***

In 1983, Jing was an eleventh grader. One day, she saw her mother open a package postmarked Canada.

"What's that?" she asked.

"A collection of short fiction from my friend."

"May I have a look?" Jing took the book and read, "*The Oldest Man and other Timeless Stories* by William Watts."

"My friend said William is a writer of children's books. If you want to read it I can help you. You can also use my English dictionary."

"Okay, my teacher, Mother." Jing stood up straight and raised her right hand to the side of her head in a military salute.

With the assistance of her mother, Jing finished reading her first book in English. One of the stories was about a butterfly collector who did not know if he was a man or a butterfly. Another story explored the thought of the famous ancient Chinese philosopher, Zhuang Zi. Jing enjoyed these fabulous stories, because each took her to a wonderful fantasy world.

Two years later, Jing attended the biology program at Beijing University. That same year, William published his thirty-second book for children.

***

On a June morning in 2003, in Guangzhou, the fragrance of the locust blossom wafted in the air under the warm sunlight after a rain. In a corner of South Paradise Park, a two-year-old boy climbed up the ladder to the slide under an aged locust tree, joyful but unsure of his footing. Jing, the child's mother, noticed there were hundreds of tiny caterpillars on the stair handrail. She looked up at the tree and saw a net hanging off some branches. Clinging to each net-thread was a caterpillar, reminding her of that article, "You Are a Worm," she had read so many years before. The breeze blew through the branches, and she seemed to hear all the worms chant, "I am a worm. You are a worm."

That same afternoon in Fredericton, New Brunswick, the delicate scent of tulips could be detected before sunset. It had just stopped raining. Alongside a path, rows of spruce trees seemed to get greener with each second that passed. Millions of spruce budworms that had survived several insecticides over numerous generations grew tougher and tougher. It seemed as though all the caterpillars were having a get-together under the trees. Pesticide spraying had decreased over the years. So the worms were able to enjoy the peace gained by the sacrifice of older generations.

The worms, hanging from thousands of threads, swung with the breeze beneath the branches. They dreamt of changing into moths. They could hear chants from a far-away land. Cheerfully, they began to sing the following choruses:

Breezes blow in spring
Spruce trees are green
Up and down with the wind
We are singing on swings.

You are humans
We are worms
We are both living things
Insecticides harm all beings.

We have survived

The deadly spraying
After the rain
Let's dance and sing.

A rainbow arched in the clear sky shimmering rays of pale blue, green, red, and gold. Children laughed excitedly, pointing at the rainbow as they ran and played in the park. Their cheers joined the song of the worms that basked in the warmth of the afternoon sun.

ACKNOWLEDGEMENTS

I AM MOST GRATEFUL to Luciana Ricciutelli, my editor at Inanna Publications and Education Inc. This short fiction collection could not have been published without her interest in my writing, her editing skills, and her insightful comments.

I also wish to thank the Toronto Arts Council for its grant assistance to my writing.

My thanks also go to my critique pals: Marlene Ritchie, Manda Djinn, Penni Stuart, and Cora J. Morace, who read all the stories in their earlier versions and provided me with their honest and useful feedback. Thank you as well to Kenneth A. MacKinnon and Li Zeng who also read some of these stories in the very early stages and encouraged me to continue writing.

Last, but certainly not least, I am grateful to my husband, Jean-Marc, and to my son, Shu, for their patience and unfailing support of my work.

Photo: Rosalind Song

Born in China, *Zoë S. Roy* was an eyewitness to the red terror under Mao's regime. Her short fiction has appeared in *Canadian Stories* and *Thought Magazine*. She holds an M.Ed. in Adult Education and an M.A. in Atlantic Canada Studies from the University of New Brunswick and Saint Mary's University. She currently lives in Toronto where she works as an adult educator. *Butterfly Tears* is her first published book.

Recycled
Supporting responsible use
of forest resources
www.fsc.org Cert no. SGS-COC-003153
© 1996 Forest Stewardship Council

Marquis Book Printing Inc.

Québec, Canada

2009

This book has been printed on 100% post consumer
waste paper, certified Eco-logo and processed chlorine free.